A Celtic Darkness

Supernatural Tales Of Ireland

By
Eoghain Hamilton

Béal Átha'n Ghaorthaidh, Cork, Ireland
Cló Litríocht
2011

Best wishes.

[signature]

Published by Cló Litriocht

Though some of the locations in these works are real, the characters and events portrayed in these stories are purely fictional. Any resemblance to any living person is purely coincidental.

Cover Designer and Graphic Artist Martin Owens, assisted by Kayla Brown

Printed in Ireland

For the light in the Darkness

Contents

Introduction

In West Cork, there is an old saying meant for anyone meeting a fairy woman on the road at night. "Bíodh an Lá agatsa agus an oíche againne" – "You have the day and we have the night".

It is wise advice to the inexperienced traveller who may have wandered inadvertently into the path of something strange. It tells us to leave well alone. That the night belongs to the spirits of the Otherworld and we humans are unwelcome. The country people in Ireland believed in such things as Banshees and Ghosts and creatures of the night. Many still do.

I have often found myself walking the country roads in Cork at all hours of the night. On the road you are alone, alone with your thoughts, your feelings and more often than not, fears. These fears are heightened by the uncertainty of being abroad on a deserted road. Each moonbeam casts a disturbing shadow. Each movement from the night-creatures in the hedgerows leaves the silence shaken and sets your mind ablaze with images of some terror lurking just beyond your vision. Your body responds, you can feel your heart beat. The back of your neck tingles and all the while you doubt. The darkness casts doubt over everything.

This collection of short stories was born in that moment of doubt. That dreadful feeling of uncertainty that walking at night on an Irish country road can bring, an uncertainty that casts a myriad of "what ifs" in your mind. Walk the road with me a while, I could use the company. Together maybe we can find out if "they" really do have the night.

Acknowledgements

Nothing is ever achieved on one's own. This collection of short stories couldn't have been created without a lot of help, encouragement and outright love from a number of people. Thanks to my wife Mary Hamilton for just being you, the greatest Anam Cara a man could wish for. A heartfelt thank you to Eileen Margerum for some fantastic support and suggestions, this collection would never have seen the light of day if it was not for your steadfast belief in me. To Professor Rod Kessler for helping me learn the craft and providing editing skills over and above any call of duty. Thanks also to Nancy Skarmeas for being patience personified in her role as primary editor. To Martin Owens for amazing cover art and design, you have forgotten more about graphic art, design and computers in general than I could hope to remember. A big thank you to Tom Fitzgerald and Paul Bailey at Cló Litriocht for getting this project to final publication. To my family and friends and anyone else who has helped along the way, thank you so very much. I should also thank the land that inspires me. Ireland, my homeland across the sea. Your haunted landscape, lonely bohreens and ancient ruins never fail to whisper new mysteries to my ear. Long may you continue to do so.

Finally, this collection is dedicated to my son Fionn Hamilton, the "fair one" you are the light in this Celtic Darkness.

Eoghain Hamilton
April 2011

Auld Lang Syne

I've been this way for many years. When I was growing up in Ireland during my teens, my father bought me a racing bike and I cycled to the movies on Friday nights. I loved the night, the darkness a velvet cloak that covered everything as I cycled the country lanes into town. The night is a blank canvas where anything and everything is possible; at night things are different, new.

I didn't bother with the lamp my father gave me to light my way. He had insisted on my using it and, while I had no wish to do myself any harm, I reckoned I could "see" more when I had it switched off. You see "seeing" is what I was looking for. I've always wanted to connect with what was out there in the mystery of the night, proof if you like that I was not alone in the world.

Cycling through the Irish countryside at night inspires a certain wonder, a fascination that can take over your thoughts. It did mine. It fed my yearning for the supernatural. I came to believe that some night, through some fortunate turn of events. I would have my proof after all.

As I grew older, I spent more time searching for the supernatural in the darkness. I walked at strange hours in all weathers, in old villages and towns, old graveyards and castle ruins to find out if "something" was out there. Often I had the feeling that something was with me; in fact, every time I wandered, I was sure I did not walk alone. Sometimes I was scared, sometimes strangely comforted. Yet, I never saw anything or found any proof that I was anything else but alone.

That was in my youth. Marriage, family and the day to day responsibilities of life have long since dulled my appetite for the Otherworld, and yet I felt the old yearnings once again as I crossed the bridge below my childhood home for the first time in many years.

The old house, the house where I had grown, was silhouetted against the night sky, a two-storied square construction, with a grand design like the Irish country houses of the aristocracy. A large portico at the front stood proudly overlooking the long driveway. Many of its rooms had windows that overlooked the river valley below. The house had been built in an attempt to blend in with some of the older houses in the vicinity, and yet it had never matched their splendour. Instead my old home had a uniqueness that demanded attention day or night.

I had been summoned from America where I had moved years earlier, by the strangest of events, a phone call in the middle of the night that woke me from a troubled sleep. I answered but the line went dead. The caller I.D placed that call from my parent's house. I thought this strange, since the house was empty, my parents having died a few years before. The next day I called my sister. She told me that the house was in between tenants, and as I expected, empty. So who had called? Who had reached out across the Atlantic to wake my feverish mind and arouse my old curiosities once again?

So I booked a flight to Shannon. My wife was annoyed since our plans for New Years Eve were disrupted, yet she understood. She always does with me.

I arrived on New Years Eve and decided not to tell my sister. An old house key that Dad had given me when I was in my teens let me in. The house felt cold; it had that damp unlived in smell which turned my nostrils. I got to work quickly and built a roaring fire, then turned on the heating, saying a short prayer that some oil left was still in the old fuel tank outside. Da had always been a miser with the oil in winter.

I made up a bed in my parent's old room. It was a room of memories. It had been many things, including my mother's death bed. Now, it would be a place to sleep – I hoped its memories would somehow comfort me.

A few hours later, I sipped cocoa and stared into the roaring log fire while I rang in the New Year. Mam was on my mind. I could almost hear her singing in the kitchen as she cooked a winter's meal on what seemed like many lifetimes ago. Then the disease struck her, and the house itself seemed to grow sick. It mirrored her deterioration, ceiling cracks and leaks all to the tune of the feverish illness of my dying Ma. My thoughts were interrupted when the house phone rang and my wife and I spent the next fifteen minutes wishing each other a happy new year. I twisted the cord as we spoke. I was restless, anxious to get back to the fire and my memories. I said goodbye and returned to the living room. In the nearby village, fireworks were cracking and illuminating the night, their loud bangs interrupting my flow of thoughts again. Afterwards, my mind cleared and I soon dozed by the fire.

A crackling spark from a smouldering log brought me back to my senses; I drove my heel against it, sending a cloud of its brothers up the flue. With a sudden tingle on my neck, the night called to me as it had so many times before. The old thrill was rising to greet me again. Was this the night? After all these years would some truth be revealed to me? I decided to see.

I switched off the lights and, closing the front door, stumbled on the newly formed ice on the patio. Luckily, I held my balance. I took a walk down the lanes around my home. It was one o'clock on a freezing New Year's morning. The newspapers had been right – snow was general all over Ireland, and a brilliant moon lit the frosty bohreen ahead. It shone with an eldritch incandescence that I hadn't witnessed in years. Moonlight is an endangered substance in the orange afterglow of the man-made cities of North America. But this moonlight was special, its brightness illuminating everything in view. I had a clear road ahead, so onward I walked, into the night.

Back in college I had read a lot about Celtic mythology. The Celts believed that at certain times of the year the veil between this world and the next grew thin and the Otherworld could be experienced in our own. Such festivals as Samhain and Bealtaine had always fascinated me. According to Celtic belief, on these nights the spirits of the dead had free reign over the earth and came back to haunt the living. I wondered if New Years and Christmas and all their trappings were something similar.

According to Dickens, Jacob Marley seemed to think so.

I walked on, lost in the memories of long ago. I thought of magical Christmases spent with my uncle's family, the two families gathered round the table on Christmas day. I thought of the happy memories of youth, wandering for hours with my friends over the fields and fishing along the riverbank. My first love, Brenda, came to mind and our first kiss on a night not unlike tonight. My father's delight when Seanie the postman brought the letter of my acceptance into university. I can still see Seanie coming up the driveway, a happy skip in his step and a knowing grin. I was a lucky man to have such memories.

A breath of cold wind brings me back to the present and I continue. The air is still now and an unusual feeling of dread comes over me. I feel dizzy, lost in my thoughts. It feels like a hidden purpose lies behind all this. A planned series of events has led me here to this junction.

I look around me for the umpteenth time for the sight I have waited for for so long. But nothing jumps from the darkness, no spirit or wraith comes forth – and yet I am tinged with sadness. A dog howls in the distance, a strange forlorn howl, I think, "You and me both, mate." A little later the road becomes icy, and I have to watch where I walk. I walk on the grassy verge of the road, and my feet crunch the frosty grass underneath making, a hollow scraping sound.

A gust of wind touches my face. I'm not far from home now, I seem to have wandered full circle on the ring road that loops around my home. It is time to get out of the cold. Besides, nothing mysterious has revealed itself to me. It is always the same. There never is anything out here in the dark, only unfulfilled promise.

Just before the short hill to the house, I stop on the humped-back bridge to listen to the river flowing underneath. How often on Halloween I have stopped here and listened to what I thought was laughter from the swollen currents underneath. I envisioned Selkies come from the Otherworld to take me back to their abode. Is that the same laughter again? Is my mind making the same mistakes it made years ago? Is this the night? Why now after all these years? I'm listening, looking, yet no female face rises before me. The sound continues! It is joined by a strange keening that fills the night air. It seems to come from the very air itself. In the distance above my home, I hear the same animal's lonely cry in the dark. I look up to my house aloft on the hill. There are lights on! I left no lights on when I came out for the walk! No cars passed me by on this the only access road. Someone was home.

So here I am, standing at the entrance to my child-hood home – and inside every light is on, the house is ablaze with lights. They blind me and I squeeze my eyes shut. Against my retina I still see their glare, a circular yellow ball, set in a sea of darkness. But wait – the yellow is widening crowding out the black. One by one I see all the memories I've forgotten. Recovered memories, hidden pains that strike hammer like against the temple of my consciousness. Da, drunk and lashing the coal shovel off my brother's face, my sister and I screeching, crying with fright, cowering in the corner of our living room. Mam's plaintive wail from as she begs Padre Pio to save Uncle Michael after his fall, from the ruin of an old castle. Brenda silhouetted against a golden August evening, raging and telling me to go and kill myself, that she doesn't care any more. James's leering grin as he thrusts into her again and again in the back of his car. The two brothers from Limerick taking turns to smack my head on the pavement. My Dad, standing by my hospital bed and stubbornly refusing to do anything about it.

The unbidden memories explode over and over. They are here. The ghosts I've looked for. I no longer need to search the night for them. They walk with me, they surround me, they have followed me everywhere I've gone. And now that I know that they are here, they will always be with me. I am a haunted man.

I stand there, the driveway stretched out before me. The memories recede for now, yet they are still faintly visible in my memory.

The lights! The lights I had switched off are still on! They shine upon me, and the glare behind the curtains of our old living room helps me to see familiar shadows within. Their forms make familiar shapes, laughing, dancing even hugging one another. I can hear the murmur of conversation, a ripple of laughter. Someone is singing "Auld Lang Syne" above the din. I have waited so very long for this. It is time to go in.

The People of Peace

"A Leannan Sidhe, she said to me. Can you believe that, Brother Finn?" Father Donahue's face was red from the effort. "I know I've dealt with some crazies before, and God knows the drugs being the way they are, we have plenty nowadays, but in all fairness, a Leannan Sidhe!"

"Did you get a look at her?" asked Brother Finn.

"I could barely make her out through the grill of the confessional," said Father Donahue. "But what I did see was beautiful, and she in no way resembled the junkies and winos of the parish. If anything she seemed well dressed, well spoken – even timid."

"So did you give her absolution?" asked the brother. The two men were strolling the outer perimeter wall of Mourne Abbey. It was a fine sunny evening in early May, and summer birds sang in the plush countryside of the valley below.

"I told her to get out. What else could I do? She was obviously a nutter, or high, or whatever. Either way, I've enough of that parish, I'll tell you." The priest shrugged his shoulders. "My time for dealing with Dublin's lost souls is at an end."

"Did she say any more?" asked Brother Finn. "Anything that caught your interest?"

"Her whole story caught my interest. That's why I was so angry. She told me everything, from what exactly happened to what she was thinking during her ordeal." Father Donahue sighed and sat on a low bench.

"It's the absurdity of it all, Brother Finn. How could a story be so obviously false but still leave me feeling so, so frightened! I tell you, I can still feel the cold in that confessional. I can still hear her soft lilting voice, sweet – like velvet it was, yet it held a terrible sadness."

"You know, this doesn't shock me. You're not the first priest to come here telling tales." Brother Finn knitted his eyebrows. "It seems that lately, I'm hearing nothing but strange stories. Anyway, you'd better tell me it all," said Brother Finn, his voice serious.

The two men sat down. Below in the countryside a skylark called a plaintive song, the evening sunshine dimmed, and Father Donahue, in slow earnest rhythms, began his tale.

Jemma breathed in the cool night air and shrugged her sports bag over her shoulder. She walked out of her home down the driveway to the road outside; the Bohreen, or "little road," glowed silver in the moonlight. The night was crisp and the sky clear. Above her, a three-quarter moon lit the countryside. Wood smoke carried on the gentle breeze. All evening the bonfires had been burning for the feast of St John. Jemma began her trek along the country lane; the sides of the valley to her left were littered with glowing red and orange dots coloured a deeper hue than the house lights beyond. Though it was near midnight, the fires still burned. 'Bonfire night," or "bonna night," as it is known in Cork, brought back special memories for Jemma. But those days were behind her now, her youth having faded these last dozen years. Now she resolutely walked toward Liscleary graveyard, her mind made up. On this, one of her favourite nights of the year, she would end her life.

Ahead, the lights of Cork Airport and from the city beyond turned the sky a deep crimson, contrasting starkly with the clear, moonlit sky behind. An aircraft screamed a plaintive wail over the field to her right and continued on its final approach. Soon Jemma passed a farmyard. An angry sheep dog ran out and snapped near her ankles. She didn't care. In fact, she barely noticed.

She just continued her steady pace until the dog turned away.

From Jemma there were no tears now. She felt hopeful, hopeful that this disaster she called a life would soon be over, hopeful that this pain would soon end. No one cared anyway, she thought, "It would be better if I hadn't been born." Years before she mightn't have believed this, but now it always felt like she was facing an overwhelming wall of hurt, a cloud of sadness that never passed, a black valley that never ended. But an old memory, on tonight of all nights, reminded her that once she had felt otherwise.

She remembered a bonfire night years before, her cotton dress of pale green billowing in the wind around her, and 'Da,' the father she had loved so much. The laughter in his eyes mixed with her cries of excitement when he lit the bonfire. She had squealed in delight as she'd jumped over the flames, dancing around the fire and calling for him to do the same. He did and caught her in a bear hug and whispered softly in her ear, "My lovely Jemma, you shine where you stand."

Not long now, she thought. I'll be with you soon, Da. Will you swing me round the fire like you did before? Jemma wondered if there really were anything beyond, if she'd ever see him after all these years. She missed him, she knew that much.

She could remember the exact time the sadness began – the night her father had held her aloft in his arms and kissed her goodnight. "If you're good," he said with a smile, "I'll bring you back chips after the pub." And with that he had turned to her mother and promised to be home soon. But he hadn't. Instead a drunk had run him over while he was walking home, and Jemma had never seen 'Da' again.

Now she remembered the counsellors, the doctors, the drugs and of course, the boys. It wasn't long before Jemma was known in the village as the fast girl, a reputation that suited her just fine. Men always played a role in her life, right up to her latest disaster with the very married Mark. Good old Mark, always the life and soul of the pub. The centre of every joke, of every childish prank, and always the "go to" guy when there was a scandal. Good old Mark, who let his kids go to school dressed in rags while he drank in the pub, who slapped his wife around a few nights a week. Good old Mark who was in with the Guards, hence their lack of interest when he had decided to give Jemma a taste of his wife's medicine.

In the distance the graveyard came into view, its wall a darker shade of navy blue than the sky beyond. Inside, two tall pine trees stood sentinel, forever keeping watch to the west. The air glimmered ahead of her, surrounding the cemetery and casting a glowing tinge on the velvet sky. The air straddled a line across the road and reminded Jemma of the edge of a rain belt, except she could see this even though it was dark. She stood in the centre of the road admiring this sight. Whatever it was, she thought, it was something in between, neither rain nor air, neither dark nor light. As she approached, the tall headstones became visible over the boundary wall. At the back of the graveyard stood an ancient ruin. Once the "Lios of the Clerics," the church of the white friars, it was now no more than a gable wall and a pile of stones. At the front, silhouetted against the night sky, were several large white and grey limestone Celtic crosses, silently monitoring Jemma's approach.

Here lay family graves that housed generations of Ireland's dead, graves etched with names that Jemma could make out in the moonlight – Shields, O'Brien, Murphy and Leahy – local people who had seen it all and who had lived out their lives. Natural selection, thought Jemma. She entered the graveyard and headed for the back, behind the ruins of the ancient chapel. Here, in the oldest section of graves, stood an old oak tree, its limbs wizened and gnarled from the unforgiving wind roaring down the Owenabui valley, its deep girth fed on the dampness of the soil and nourished on the human flesh beneath.

Jemma sat and opened her bag. She pulled out the bottle of Vodka and the vial of sleeping pills and wasted no time in swallowing four or five, washing them down with a swig from the bottle. The liquid burned her throat, but she ignored the discomfort and did the same again, this time swallowing a fist full of pills. The hard part was next. She gathered her strength and then resolutely she reached in and took the Swiss army knife from her bag. Rolling up her coat sleeve, she opened the knife and, as quickly as she could, made a horizontal cut into her wrist. She grimaced in pain, then felt a hot gush as her veins opened and the blood spilled onto on her knife hand. It flowed in a fast stream down into the soil, where it would mingle with what lay beneath. And now, she thought, some blessed relief.

Jemma sat back again and felt the life drain from her body. A sense of calm shrouded her. A soft wind caressed the graveyard and gently swayed the high growth of midsummer. She surveyed the ancient ruins one last time, then looked up into the night sky. Billions of stars sparkled in the clear air. Their beauty gave Jemma a sense of hope. She felt the first pangs of drowsiness and inwardly smiled. It was beginning.

After a time, the stars began to shift and move, first one, then many, until finally cascades of stars shot through the heavens. They ran and ran across the night sky, leaving a trail of light behind them. Jemma was attracted into their movement as the lights of billions of dancing stars dipped and changed, moving both swiftly and slow. Her mind was tugged towards them, a mental reaching to touch the universe. She felt a pull in their direction, something drawing her toward them.

The lights continued to shimmer and change. Then they began to gather; first a tiny star joined another at the centre of the sky, then another and another, slowly building up into one large star. The star continued to grow, filling the night sky and bathing the graveyard in light. Jemma was warmed and touched by the light, and she smiled at its beauty and comfort. The light was blinding, but still Jemma looked on. From somewhere deep within the light three small figures walked toward her. Eventually, Jemma distinguished three female forms. The figures came closer, their forms blurring and changing and merging into one. An old woman finally stood within the light before Jemma. She held an ornate cup in her hand, and with a faint smile on her wrinkled, kindly face she offered it to Jemma.

"Drink this and live forever," said the kindly old woman.

Jemma lifted the cup and smiled, and then she drank deeply. The liquid was delicious. Its coolness seemed to calm the ache in her soul. Then ecstasy flooded through her. Her ears were filled with the sweetest music. Her mind flooded with luscious poetic thoughts. She looked around her and felt the beauty in this ancient graveyard and throughout the land beyond, its energy hitting her like a giant pulse. She looked for the old woman, but in her place stood the most beautiful young woman she had ever seen. Jemma rose, tears cascading down her cheeks. "Thank you, our lady," she sobbed, "Thank you for this release."

The young maiden took Jemma by the hand and turned her to face the north. Instead of the Owenabui valley, a giant grassy mound with a narrow stone-cut entrance lay before her.

"Come with me, my child," said the figure. "I have much to show you." They walked hand in hand inside, Jemma's consciousness still swimming at what she was seeing. The mound was hollow, and it opened up into a wide hallway where what seemed like thousands of people waited to see the two enter.

The maiden spoke again. "Behold, my child – the people of peace, generations of Ireland's dead since the dawn of time."

Jemma looked at the thronging crowd of white-faced people and thought she recognized faces she knew from the village in her youth.

"These are my children," said the maiden. "Some served me well in the older times."

Jemma looked around the figures she was now beginning to recognize. There was uncle Michael! And Timmy Lyons, the old man from the corner shop. But where was her father?

"Some of my children," the woman continued, "I have asked to die for Ireland." The woman's features grew older before Jemma's eyes. "Some of my children," the woman spoke again, her features becoming older and more corrupted as Jemma gazed on, "I have asked to leave my land so that the name of our island would be known forever." The woman became a creature now rotten and decrepit, flesh peeling from her face, skin falling in folds and dropping to the floor at her feet. Jemma backed away. She turned toward the crowd and caught a sight she had not seen in years. A tall well-built man stood with his back to her, but she knew that hair.

"Da, Daddy, it's me." She reached through the crowd grasping for the father she loved so much. "Daddy, turn 'round! It's your Jemma." The man began to turn. From behind, Jemma heard the rotten creature call.

"But you, my child, my child who has suffered, who has lived in sadness and without hope, you will FEED for Ireland."

Hundreds of arms reached out and took hold of Jemma. They grabbed every part of her in an iron grip. She fought as much as she could, stretched her arms forward and screamed, "Daaaaadeeeeeeeeeeeeeee!"

The man in the crowd turned and recognition flooded his face. He reached towards her but she was carried aloft among the crowd and back towards the entrance of the mound. Through the blizzard of arms and faces of the dead she saw her father mouth the word "Jemma."

Jemma woke in the graveyard, the creature standing before her. Her body felt the coldest she had ever felt in her life, her wrist throbbed and her heart ached for the father she loved; yet she began to sense new things. She heard a rustling in the field beyond and instantly knew it was a field mouse. She could smell the decayed flesh in the earth. From a house a few fields away came the most wonderful smell. It drew her and called to her and made her body shiver. It gave her the most incredible thirst she had ever felt.

The creature looked upon Jemma with malevolence in her yellow eyes. "I condemn you to wander this island in darkness, to feed upon human kind," she said, bending low to bring its rotten face closer. "You will walk between the living and the dead and will feed upon the irreverent. You will be a portent of the great sorrow that is to come. Yours is now a life eternal, a search unending for human blood."

Jemma, now delirious, screamed and screamed. She kicked and flailed her body like a mad woman, but the figure simply turned and shuffled out of the graveyard. Jemma howled after her, after her father, after her life.

"And that was her tale, Brother Finn," said Fr. Donahue, his voice shaking. "She told me she has wandered the country since, sleeping in old barns, in ruined cottages and of course in ancient tombs. She told me she has fed upon the living the length and breadth of the country."

"Have you seen her since?" asked Brother Finn.

"Every night. She haunts my dreams and my waking thoughts are filled with her story...yet logic tells me she was just another whacked-out junkie."

"I don't think you believe that, do you?" Brother Finn asked incredulously.

"What am I to believe, Brother? I know of the two farmers missing in Cork, of that plumber – what was his name, Mark Byrne – that was found at the bottom of a quarry!" cried the now tearful priest. "But logic tells me it can't be true."

"What will you do now?" asked brother Finn.

"I don't know, Brother. This is my third retreat in as many weeks. And wherever I go she haunts my dreams. Even here in my bed she haunts me. My mind is full of stories, of song, of the most amazing poetry, of thoughts and ideas I never thought possible. I feel weaker by the day. It's that cold, Brother Finn. It shrouds me. It touches me to the very bone. I shall never get over it."

Gaoth Sidhe

"Hello, Mr. Levis?" Sorry to call you so late. My name is Eamon Costello. I'm doing research on Dralane Castle for a book of tales I'm writing about the old houses of South Cork. Regarding the Castle, I was wondering if you knew any of the folklore?"

"How much time have you got, my boy?" It was an old man's voice on the line.

"Sorry?"

"Mr. Costello, I'm nearly eighty years old. My family has known the Villers of Dralane for many generations - of course I know many of the legends surrounding the old place. Much of the lore was passed on to me by my father. I could keep you on the phone all night."

"Oh, sorry, Mr. Levis. Could I come and see you? Would sometime tomorrow be OK?"

"Call round at three, Mr. Costello, and I'll tell you the tale of Francis Villers. The story is about a hundred years old now. You won't be disappointed."

The next day, in the sitting room of Geroge Levis's old house, surrounded by generations of memento's from other ages, the old man recounted his strange tale...

Francis Villers was the kindliest Anglo that any man in the vicinity of south Cork was lucky enough to meet. His family seat was at Dralane on the outskirts of Carrigaline. It was a square Normanesque tower constructed on a rocky limestone outcrop overlooking the Owenabui River. After the Elizabethan conquest, the old McCarthy clan suffered attainment, and the castle fell into the hands of the Villers family. It has remained so ever since.

Towards the end of the last century, Francis returned from India following the death of his rather dislikeable father. Francis had served with the Munster Fusiliers and had fought in the Punjab rebellion some years before. Wounded through the leg and suffering from a lingering infection, he had bravely served out his commission and returned to Dralane a changed spirit. It was often said that the difference between him and his father the previous Lord of Dralane was night and day. For Francis, having seen enough of war and suffering in the deserts of India, had decided to do his best for his fellow man and particularly for the tenants on the estate. It was for this reason that Francis was loved by many of his neighbours far and wide in the southern part of County Cork.

He was also a patient and courteous man. It was once said that when his company was requested at a Queenstown regatta by the retired Admiral Wolsey, an old friend of his father's, Francis had patiently endured the old eccentric's ramblings for a number of days until the festivities had ended and tired, of racing Galway Hookers around Cork harbour, the gentle Francis had escorted the rear admiral to his hotel suite, bidding him farewell. Without another sidestep or detour in his path, he had returned to Dralane once again.

For it was at Dralane that Francis was happiest. He loved the estate and worked it constantly. He was always up to some endeavour or other. He spent hours scouring the farmer's almanac for better farming methods. He constantly monitored the cattle herd for signs of disease or sickness, and he was forever making improvements to the castle and the adjoining buildings.

To his tenant's delight, he restored the ruined gable wall of the old Cistercian abbey that had long ago operated on the boundaries of his estate, and he cleared the nearby Holy Well of Bride that had become overgrown after years of neglect. On a bright May morning, the local Catholic priest, standing in a sea of bluebells that carpeted the earth around the well, held mass and rededicated the well to St. Bride. Days of merriment followed, and none were so pleased as were the local tenants with the new Lord of Dralane. When asked about the matter, he replied that he had felt it was "the right thing to do." He was a most conscientious landlord, a diligent and utterly hard working man.

Not long after he restored the old well, Francis was visited by an archaeologist from University College Cork. Dr Patrick Ryan, the academic, was a well known authority on castles built in the mid 1500's by the Gaelic clans of old. He was particularly knowledgeable of those erected by the McCarthy Clan of Cloghroe, including Dralane Castle and their more famous production at Blarney. The two men walked the grounds of the castle together and, during a conversation that lasted a number of hours, Professor Ryan informed Francis of his belief that several tunnels had been cut into the limestone outcrop on which Dralane Castle was built. He requested permission to carry out limited excavation in the base-ment to ascertain if these tunnels existed and might be accessed. While Francis agreed with the archaeologist that there might be tunnels underneath Dralane, since any castles worth their salt at the time had a number of escape routes underneath, he wholeheartedly disagreed about excavation. He flatly refused, pointing out that they weren't his ancestors buried there, and that whatever lay underneath Dralane could stay buried. Francis, much in agitation, added that he was concerned with the prosperity of the land above rather than the fortunes of whatever lay beneath.

The professor implored Francis to carry out the investigation, mentioning his belief that during the final siege of Dralane, members of the McCarthy clan might have been pursued and massacred in the tunnels by English troops. The doctor thought that the fleeing escapees may have been carrying certain "last minute" artefacts. In exasperation, he threw his hands in the air saying, "Who knows what we might find?" But Francis would not be swayed. He wanted to see the past buried and forgotten, and he said, with a new century fast approaching, it was time that Dralane, Ireland, and Britain as a whole built a prosperous future. At length, Dr Ryan gave up and returned to the university, mindful of a missed opportunity.

Not long after, Francis met Lady Elizabeth Townsend of Skibbereen. After a brief engagement the two married and started a family. The fact that she was an only child herself encouraged her towards a large family. She often stated that she wanted to "have many children around her." In time, the castle grew too small for the increasing

Villers family, and after a brief deliberation on how to proceed, Francis decided to add a new wing.

The work on the foundations began in the spring of 1899, on the very eve of the new century. The work was slow. Much of the limestone outcrop on which Dralane was perched continued underneath the proposed addition, the result being that local labourers were forced to break rock to carve out a suitable foundation. While working in a particularly deep and difficult trench, a local man, O'Brien, drove his pick axe through a chunk of bedrock, embedding it. On withdrawing the axe with great effort, he loosened a slab about half a foot wide. O'Brien, in that instant, was blown out of the trench by what can only be described as an enormous burst of air gusting from below. When it stopped, the workmen re-entered the trench and found a hole in the bedrock. Below, the space was hollow. The workmen dropped stones into the hole which quickly disappeared before a short tap could be heard where the stone had struck the floor somewhere beneath. Francis ordered the remaining men to expose the hole further, and by the day's end, Dr. Ryan's theories about tunnels underneath Dralane had been proved correct. The opening was widened to about three feet square and a ladder was put down, reaching the cavern floor some ten feet below. The cave was left overnight, to allow any foetid air to escape, and the next day Francis was the first to take a look.

It was a bright June morning as Francis descended; the light he carried gave off a faint yellow tint that reflected the from limestone cavern beneath. Francis's feet touched the cavern floor and the light disappeared from view when he moved beyond the range of sight to examine the rooms beneath. He was gone for some time, no doubt exploring some of the ancient tunnels.

At length a pale and frightened-looking Francis Villlers scrambled up out of the hole and ordered the men to withdraw the ladder. In a panic, he screeched for the foundation to be filled in that very day. Concerned, the workmen who knew him well, asked him what he'd seen, but he ignored their requests and ordered them to continue filling in the footings. The work was abandoned. Within a day the opening was sealed and the new foundations were once again filled in.

Over the following weeks, Francis grew morose and aloof. He roamed the grounds alone and often walked the fields after dark. In time he regained some of his old self and by New Years was drawing up plans to construct a new wing on the other side of the castle. During that winter he received a letter from Professor Ryan, who had heard of the incident and who was once again entreating

Francis to carry out the archaeological survey. The request was promptly refused.

The following Spring, work began, and by late October the new wing was ready, its towering walls rising to meet the battlements of the old fortress itself. Indeed, Francis had specifically designed the new building so that he could walk both the old and the new rooftop battlements together. Francis and Elizabeth, being so delighted with their new living quarters, invited their friends from nearby estates to come to a Halloween party. It was an unusually warm October that year, and as the last day on the month dawned, a golden sun shone on the harvested fields around Dralane.

Preparations for the evening were in full swing. The kitchen at Dralane was helter skelter, and the smell of roast meat and fruit pies pervaded the castle. Francis had procured the services of old Michelin O'Dailigh, the famous fiddler of Kinsale, to entertain the gathering, and a number of the tenants had decided to line the avenue to Dralane with torches to welcome the guests. As the first carriages arrived after nightfall, they were treated to a impressive sight of a torch-lit avenue, while the sound of a piper reverberated across the fields to greet them. It was to be a happy occasion.

The evening was a wonderful success, the dinner a masterpiece and the music and dancing performed in such a way that only those who have known Ireland can truly understand. Francis was in full flow, regaling the guests with humorous tales of his sailing exploits with the retired Admiral Wolsey. Outside, the tenants lit a marvellous bonfire to celebrate the evening, and the diners enjoyed an after-dinner stroll in the night air. It was an opportunity to savour the atmosphere and music at the bonfire.

Towards midnight the bonfire sank to low embers, and many of the tenants tapered off to their cabins, no doubt in preparation for work the next day. With only half of the crowd remaining and the celebrations well and truly ebbing, it being November Eve, a call arose for Nan Casey to tell one of her famous ghost stories. Nan was the local Seanachai for the parish, and she was known throughout Carrigdhoun, West Cork, and as far away as Kerry as a storyteller of fine repute. So, as the embers of the bonfire flickered, Nan wrapped her shawl tightly about her and began her tale.

"Twas long ago now, when the English soldiers came to Dralane, a week or so after the defeat of O'Neil at Kinsale. O'Neil's army was scattered throughout south Cork in retreat from that English blackguard Mountjoy.

The McCarthys cowered in their castle here at Dralane, awaiting the terrible retribution of the English. On a Halloween morning much like the one we had today, the English arrived. They surrounded the castle and soon discovered the exits to the escape tunnels in the meadow beyond. Quickly, the English barricaded them up. I need not tell you of what took place then, for we all know of that terrible day when the Gael perished at Dralane. But what is not known is that McCarthy's son, little Donnach Og, hid in the basement of the castle and attempted to make his escape in the tunnels beneath. Little five-year-old Donnach was a brave boy. He brought into the dark tunnels underneath Dralane, a lantern, and the knife his father had given him on his last birthday. When Mount-joy's business was done outside, the English commander went indoors to plunder the castle for its family treasures, and soon enough the entrance to the tunnels was discovered in the castle basement. But rather than risk themselves in the dark, the English, like the cowards they were, walled up the entryway.

Lost in the tunnels underneath, little Donnach wandered those cold limestone caverns until his light went out. There he sat in the dark waiting his end. A bright child, he knew there was no escape, so instead of crying for his mother and father he called for the Good

People to come for him. For he remembered how his mother had told him that the Good People would sometimes come to the aid of those in need. He called and called in the dark for the fairies, for the Pooka, for Una, the family Beansidhe, to take him away with them to their world where he could remain forever a prince among them. No one knows what happened after that. Little Donnach Og was never found, but it was often said by the old people when I was a young girl that on November Eve, if you walked around the rock of Dralane and listened very carefully, you would hear the faint sound of a little boy bravely calling on the wind for his fairy kinsmen to come to him."

A short snap of a breeze rushed through the gathering and broke Nan Casey's spell. The crowd gave a collective shudder; a few nervous laughs and snatches of conversation arose. The ghost story over, the crowd dispersed, and one by one Francis's guests bade him good night. It was remarked later that Francis looked pale and wide-eyed and said good night to his guests in a distracted, distant manner.

Francis slept fitfully through the night. His dreams were feverish, he muttered in his sleep, and at one stage, he cried out. Lady Elizabeth even heard him pleading in his nightmarish dreams. On waking at around three in the morning, he told his wife that he was feeling ill and was going up to the battlements to take some air. Elizabeth drifted toward sleep while she listened to the gentle footfalls on the stone cut stairs outside their room.

Several minutes later an enormous burst of wind shook the castle foundations. It was a terrible blast. Later it was found to have ripped many of the thatched roofs from the houses at Carrigaline. A wild, inhuman shriek sounded from above. Lady Elizabeth screamed and ran for the battlements. But on gaining the rooftop, she could not find Francis. The servants soon followed and made a thorough search of the castle and the surrounding grounds, but Francis was nowhere to be seen.

At daylight, a search party and dogs searched the surrounding woods. That afternoon they found Francis impaled on branch of an old oak tree forty feet above the ground; impossibly, he was half a mile beyond the castle in a copse of ancient oak and ash by the river. O'Brien, the same man that had been blown out of the trench, climbed the tree and to his amazement found that Francis was still alive, semi-conscious and in terrible pain. A doctor was called who on examination found that there was nothing that could be done. He administered some pain medication to ease Francis's discomfort, and a distraught Lady Elizabeth was brought to the scene to say goodbye to her husband. Her sorrow was terrible to behold, but bravely she took hold of the rope and was raised aloft to her husband. There, she kissed him fondly, his blood all the while staining her dress. In anguish, he raised her face to his and mouthed something in her ear. She nodded and gently placed his forehead back upon her shoulder. After several moments and several anguished gasps upon the breast of his loving wife, he died.

Francis was buried on a windswept November day, the whole village turning out to say goodbye. He was laid to rest in the churchyard at De Lyon's rock, and several keeners were heard long into the night mourning his passing.

A year later, Dr Ryan of University College Cork was granted leave by Lady Elizabeth to excavate the tunnels. The opening that the workmen had exposed was soon uncovered, and an excited Dr Ryan descended into the darkness as Francis had on that May morning. After wandering among the caverns, Dr Ryan was astounded to find an alcove in which lay the skeletal remains of a child. The cold had preserved the clothing, which looked to be Elizabethan in style. At the child's hand was the rusty remains of an old knife, and what looked like a lantern lay by his side. Around his neck was a large stone pendant in the shape of a tear drop. Ryan removed the trinket and was surprised to find that it could be opened. Inside was a cloth pouch. Ryan took the pouch to the university to be examined. On opening the pouch, a thinly rolled parchment lay within and written on the parchment was a short verse in old Irish. When translated it read,

We heard your call and came to take you to the wilds
where you would be a prince among the people of the isles,
but death had gone before us and spirited you away,
so here we'll wait in darkness till the living come someday
and with a stroke of Fairy wind, those above shall pay.

And that was really that, Mr Costello. The remains of the little boy were buried with his kinsmen at Blarney and beneath the castle the tunnels were sealed up, Professor Ryan's dig had found that there was no more to be discovered at Dralane."

"Good God, Mr Levis, what a terrible story. That poor boy. Is it really true?"

"Absolutely! The records are at the university and are there for all to see. Poor Francis, he suffered such an agonizing death."

"What killed him, Mr Levis? How did he manage to end up half a mile away impaled on an ancient oak tree?"

"Well, I've only heard the stories, mutterings if you like. The old women used to talk about such a thing. In

Irish they called it the Gaoth Sidhe, a fairy wind. The women used to say it was a terrible thing, a weapon of the Otherworld. It was, they said, a wind so powerful that once it was released, it could never be stopped and it would take anything in its path."

The Summer House

"All things give themselves yet none may take." - Eva Goore Booth

The journey seemed to take forever. Only now, after six hours of driving, did Ryan reach the town of Killarney, not far from the Kerry border. He had at least another half an hour to go to Killbeigh, and he could hardly keep his eyes open. Pulling into McDonalds for a well-earned coffee and a rest, Ryan sighed at the sight of the empty streets. Killarney was a different place in mid November. Gone were the throngs of eager, enthusiastic American tourists and local Jarveys ready to fleece their victims to the last Euro. Gone were the great crowds of Munster Football final day, their scarlet and greens put away for another year, and gone were the night revellers rolling around the streets, intoxicated on their weekend escapades. In its place Killarney was a ghost town, a maze of empty streets where a cold winter wind blew litter across street lights and shop fronts. An empty vessel where the buzzing of the traffic lamps sounded between gusts of wind on this winter's night, where everyone and everything seemed in some form of hibernation.

Eventually Ryan got his coffee, loaded it with extra sugar, and drove on. It had been a long journey from Dublin. His father had suggested that he paint the McDonough's summer house. He would be paid for his effort, and the month-long project would give him time to refocus and contemplate his future. Now that Deirdre had moved out and they had both gone their separate ways, it really was time for a change. Besides, his one-year contract at Deane and Co. Engineers was up, the plans for the new road finished. So maybe it was time to heal the wounds of Deirdre and focus on his future career. Some Kerry air and a bit of exercising while painting the house would help.

Around 11 o'clock Ryan arrived at the house. He phoned his father.

"Good, you're in then," his father told him. "Ted says there are sheets in the airing cupboard, the switch for the heating is there too." A cautious tone came over his father's voice. "You'll find the paint in the shed outside, and, Ryan, don't let me down."

Hanging up the phone, Ryan found the sheets and made up his bed. The house was musty. Not a window had been opened to air the place. He walked round the house and opened all the bedroom windows. Gazing outside, he saw the back garden in the moonlight. Beyond lay a vast expanse of strand. Beyond that, the Atlantic glowed silver in the moonlight. Ryan climbed into bed and let his thoughts focus on the lapping of the gentle tide outside. He listened and began to drift. He thought of Deirdre and their final break up. The tears in her eyes when she finally decided that she had had enough. He saw the smashed coffee pot and the broken kitchenware, the aftermath of his temper once again getting the best of him. He let out a sigh as he pictured her exiting their Dublin apartment, her suitcase packed. Just as he was about to fall asleep, he thought he heard a child's giggle. He put the sound down to fatigue and within a few seconds, drifted off to sleep.

Ryan awoke feeling as he had the night before, with the sound of the ocean lapping against his ears. He looked out his bedroom window into the dark morning and felt the usual sense of melancholy that prevails throughout Ireland in November. On top of his own personal sorrow, he felt the sense of loss that only the winter can bring. Long gone were the joys of summer.

The day trippers had vanished. This holiday destination was now bare of all the summer's promise, a getaway no more.

Ryan focused his energies on the task at hand. The McDonoughs had left everything he would need for painting. He moved furniture and dropped dust sheets to protect the carpet. He cracked open a can of interior paint, pulled out his stepladder, flicked on the radio, grabbed his brush, and was off about his business.

At three in the afternoon, tired of the work, Ryan decided to finish early and explore the strand behind. The weather had turned unusually warm for November. He sweated profusely in the sunshine, walking the five miles expanse of sand. His thoughts of Dublin were momentarily forgotten. All around him the sea roared its mighty song. In the dunes he heard winter birds chirping at the passing wintry brightness. The day was in stark contrast with Killarney's gloom the night before, and Ryan wondered at the off-season atmosphere that surrounded the beach, a dreary place, pitched in this beautiful region. He thought of the laughter on the wind the night before but dismissed it as tiredness in the bright light of this day. Ahead of him a large rock loomed out of the ocean floor. It nestled on the edge of the tide, the waters lapping round to encircle the lonely bastion. Ryan walked up to the rock and observed a crevice at its centre. The middle of the rock was hollow. Wet sand covered its floor. A small skeleton lay nestled against the rock on the inner side of the crevice. When he saw it, Ryan shrieked.

"Helleo," said a voice in a strong Kerry accent. "Are you the biy staying at the shummer house?"

Ryan nearly jumped out of his skin. Behind him stood a small man around five feet four. The man seemed to have come from nowhere. "Yes, I'm helping to renovate the place." He said his name, extending his hand.

The old man took the hand a gazed at Ryan. "I see you've discovered Maire Beag," said the old man.

"Should we call anyone?" asked Ryan.

"No, no. Shur she's bin dere since de famine. Poor divil, she must have crawled here during her last hours, dying with the hunger," said the old man shaking his head. "Sometimes when the tide is low, she shows herself, then again today isn't a very low tide. All the leocal knows she's dere. Some say she even sits on the rock at night and cries. But shur dems only stories. Anyway, good luck now."

"Good luck" said Ryan, and the old man moved away with a slight gait in his step. Ryan wandered on into the distant strand, shocked at his discovery. Here he was feeling sorry for himself, and he finds this poor dead child. He thought, "and I think I have problems!"

Dinner at the nearby pub was followed by a couple of pints of cider, a perfect remedy to his mood. The landlord informed Ryan that the man he'd met was Timmy Murphy. "Timmy's a bit touched," said the man. "Not been right since the brother hanged himself years ago. He's an alcoholic now, spends most of his time at the Drimbay Tavern. When he's broke, he walks the strand or picks mussels on the rocks." The landlord smiled. "It's a wonder he didn't tap you for a few bob."

Ryan returned the landlord's smile at this, but underneath he shivered, as Timmy had seemed quite sane when they had spoken.

The next day dawned mild and clear again. Ryan took to his decorating with vigour. Sweat glistened from his brow. He sang along with the dreadful Christmas tunes that were beginning to permeate the airwaves, and he even commented mockingly on the talk show that contained its usual offering of world-weary stories and other people's suffering. By evening Ryan had once again forgotten the day before. After it had grown dark, he decided to take another walk to get some air. This time the night was black. Nothing could be seen on the shore ahead. With no moon to light his way, Ryan could hardly see his own hand in front of his face. Surprisingly, it wasn't cold and the tide seemed incredibly still. Ryan's mind wondered to the little girl on the beach. Had it been her laughter he had heard? Shrugging his shoulders, he returned to the summer house. Walking through the back garden, he clearly heard footsteps on the patio at the side of the house. He walked round to the patio, the nape of his neck going cold. Again the footsteps sounded. Ryan drew nearer.

Rounding the corner to the patio, he called, "Hello," but no one was there. Only the darkness of the night held the patio, and the lap of the tide from the beach behind gently broke the silence. From the roof above came the sound of more footsteps. The deep thump of someone walking around on the flat roof was unmistakeable. Ryan ran to the back of the house and jumped up onto the oil tank; from there he could hoist himself onto the roof. As soon as his vision cleared the flat roof-line, he saw that no one was there.

To be sure, he jumped up and walked around the old ash-felt roof. From up here the view was better. At last the moon had broken through the velvet clouds above. The distant hillsides of the Dingle peninsula glowed silver in the moonlight. He couldn't believe how spectacular they looked even at night. He was jolted back to reality by the same laughter. It echoed all around him. Ryan had had enough. Climbing down the same way he'd gone up, Ryan stormed inside and grabbed the shaft of an axe handle left behind years before. He switched on every light, looked in every bedroom. Taking a flashlight from the broom cupboard, he went outside and looked around. He even walked the narrow lanes outside for over an hour but no one could be found. Returning home to the illuminated house, he bolted the doors and windows and went to bed with the lights on.

It didn't stop the dream. In front of him the little girl was running, giggling, stumbling through the weeds and out onto the sandy beach. She was wearing what seemed like a communion dress and it billowed as it caught the sea breeze. A little boy giggled while he ran to meet her. The girl made for the large, oval shaped rock at the edge of the tide. Together the two climbed the large rock as the waters of the tide encircled them below. They weren't worried they could paddle ashore. Climbing steadily to the rock's centre, the girl stood aloft, her arms in the air. "Look!" she yelled, "I'm on the top, the top of Danger Island."

The boy laughed and scrambled after her. Suddenly a giant wall of white exploded behind the girl. Its spray blinded the boy. He couldn't see, he could just about hold onto the slimy rock on which he was perched. When his eyes cleared, he screamed and screamed for his friend. He struggled to the top, but she was gone. The freak wave had washed her away. Panic gripped the boy, he called for her and searched the ocean for her, but there was no answer. Tears welled up in his young eyes. He cried aloud and began to climb down the rock to the water. He finished his climb with a short jump, landing in the two foot of shallow water below. Immediately something tightened upon his ankle. He struggled against it, and it moved with him like a large chunk of seaweed. He pulled with all his might but still couldn't loosen its grip. He headed ashore. The weed attached to his ankle dragged with him as he broke the water's edge and touched the sand again. He pulled from the sea a lump of seaweed at least four feet long. Hoping to get help, he dropped to his ankle to tear away the weed. His hands touched something cold. Gently, he removed a large clump of weed to reveal the sleeve of the dress below. Inside the sleeve the hand was grey and wizened. It grasped his leg. The boy exploded in fright, screaming and tearing, trying to get away. But still the hand held tight on his ankle. He tore at the rest of the ball. A clump fell away to reveal the girl's corpse-like face. Despite his panic, the boy became mesmerised by her features, her grey death face pulling his eyes in. He peered over the forehead, the closed eyes, the mouth with its tongue protruding. He gazed at her grey cheeks and stared at her eyes again, the eyes opened.

"Tell them I'm coming," she said.

Ryan woke up screaming.

The next morning, shaken from the night before, Ryan skipped work and walked further along the beach than he had since his arrival. He avoided the gruesome rock, walking instead around the spit of the beach. He passed the old light tower and went onto the back strand. It was dark by the time he reached the old shipwreck, and he sat on the broken timbers in the dark thinking of his terrible dreams and his ruined affair with Deirdre. What was he to do with his life? Where was his ex now? He was just thinking of her relaxing in some Dublin apartment when the noise came. A hundred voices in his head, whispering, growing rapidly into a crescendo that nearly deafened him. They screamed into his brain, and Ryan reached for his ears. As quickly as they came, they receded back to a whisper, but they didn't leave altogether. Ryan couldn't make out what they were saying, but it didn't matter. The noise rose to a deafening level again, his eardrums thumping against the pressure.

Again the noise receded and returned again. By now Ryan had fallen from his seat, clutching his ears. He screamed as he lay in the sand.

Again the noise came, again he screamed. He looked to his left to see the waves crashing against the beach. The motion of the waves was keeping time with the rising of the noise. As soon as this thought struck him, the noise stopped, and Ryan was left alone in the sand, looking out upon the sea-foam racing ashore to meet him. Rising gingerly from the sand, Ryan put a hand to his ear. His fingers came away covered in blood. Later that night after a hot bath and a shave, Ryan lay on the sitting room sofa in front of a roaring turf fire. Lingering over an ancient copy of *Moonfleet*, he felt drowsy. Within ten minutes Ryan was asleep.

This time he was in his office in Dublin, closing his latest deal, joking and laughing with his colleagues and back slapping his boss. The laughter grew louder and louder. Then he saw each staff lean over the boardroom table, except the table wasn't a table any more. It was a giant hunk of quivering flesh. One by one the board members dipped their mouths in the flesh, chewing and laughing, blood running down their faces. His boss looked up at Ryan. "Good stuff, isn't it Ryan?" Then Ryan tasted blood on his lips.

Ryan awoke from his dream. Hot tears scalding his cheeks. Sweat bathed his body. He felt nauseated and ran to the bathroom to be sick. While he was retching, he thought he heard a faint giggle from the hallway beyond. By the time he was finished throwing up, he was too tired to care about anything. He went to bed. Soon, exhaustion took him and he fell asleep

The next day Ryan decided that he had had enough. He called his father, telling him that it was time to leave.

"But you can't," yelled his dad. "You're paid up until Christmas and besides, the work isn't finished."

"Fuck the work!" screamed Ryan. "There is something wrong with this house.

Ryan's Dad lost his temper. "Ryan, you're a disaster. I thought you'd given up the acid. What are you saying, the house is haunted? I've stayed several times. There is nothing wrong with that house."

"Well, who's the little girl, then?"

His Dad exploded. "There is no girl, there are no ghosts. And you are letting me down. Get the job finished for Bill and we'll talk then."

Ryan gave up. He said his goodbyes and hung up. He dialled the number of the local Church of Ireland minister, Eamon Proctor. The man had invited him to dinner in the pub and Ryan had decided to take him up on the offer.

Eamon was delighted to hear from him. "Certainly old boy," said the minister. "We'll see you at seven.

 "I have something to tell you," said Ryan.

" I know," said Eamon. "You're having problems in the house."

Ryan was amazed.

"Come over this evening and we'll talk."

Ryan hung up the phone, his mind whirling.

"Awful place in winter," continued the minister over his brandy. "I got a feeling there once myself. Strange but that feeling wasn't around a few years ago." The vicar knitted his eyebrows. "But in recent years, when the nights darken and the tourists desert the place, it develops some sort of atmosphere. The McDonoughs asked me to bless the place one time, and I only got as far as the kitchen when I saw a child's reflection in a window. I ran in a hurry.

Ryan was incredulous, "You ran? Aren't you supposed to be a priest?"

"True, I am, but not a very good one. Besides, they don't pay me enough to suffer that kind of stress."

"Pay," asked Ryan. "Are you mad? If there is something in the house then, you should have removed it."

"Don't you get it, boy?" said the minister. "It's not just the house. It's the place, the beach out back, the road in front, the whole area is tainted in winter. It's too big for me."

"So call the bishop," said Ryan.

"Sorry," said the minister, "the bishop and I don't really speak. You see, I'm here in this backwater thanks to a certain indiscretion with parish funds. The horses you see. Like many of my stock, I like the Gigi's."

Ryan was astounded. "Who else knows about the place"?

"Not many, just the few locals. It's avoided, so to speak."

"So basically I'm here for the winter. I can't leave, as my Dad owes old man McDonough a favour. The church can't help me, and I'm stuck in Spooksville." Ryan was wondering what else could go wrong, when the vicar spoke.

"You're too young to face this. There is deep anger in that place." He pleaded with Ryan. "Go home, go back to Dublin, where it is warm and safe. The haunted shores of Kerry are no place for a city boy like you."

"It's the child, isn't it?" said Ryan. "It's that poor little Maire Beag who wandered to the rock nearby and died during the famine."

"Yes," said the rector, "and no. Some have encountered her ghost yes, but mostly by the rock. The house is different, Ryan. leave it be. Go home."

The dinner ended without anything being resolved. Ryan returned to the summer house feeling a little light-headed after the brandy. As soon as his head hit the pillow, he was asleep.

Christmas neared, the days continued, and so, too, did the nights. Each night Ryan dreamed. One moment he was chewing the flesh in his office in Dublin, the next he was racing toward the rock, the young girl in front of him. Ryan's health deteriorated. He ate less and became weak. One day, not long before the painting was due to be completed, Timmy Murphy and an old woman appeared at his the gate.

"Willuh come round this avening for the tae?" the woman asked. "You look like you nade it."

"I will," answered Ryan, who carried on painting as if they weren't there. He knew who she was. Everyone in Killbeigh knew the old spinster who once had been a beautiful air hostess with Aer Lingus. Folk complained about her. Said she was filthy and that her house was walking with the dirt. They also said she was mad. Ryan wondered what she would have to say about the place. He wondered if she could help him get some sleep.

Ryan arrived at Meg Casey's house in a state of weariness. Neither spoke as they dined over a meatless dinner of boiled vegetables and jacket potatoes. Meg saw the distaste in Ryan's face toward the food.

"Eat your food, biy," she called to him. "Long ago we would have been glad of this. But nowadays,"she mused, "only fillet steak will do. Sur if the gentry ever came back, they'd fit right in." Then the old woman stopped abruptly, stared across the dinner table, and whispered, "You are to be visited tonight biy. Yu'll need your strength."

"What strength," he screamed. "Who is coming? What is going on in that house?" But Meg just sighed and the mad, glazed look returned to her eyes. Timmy quieted Ryan's screaming, and the dinner ended with nothing more than a cup of tea and ten minutes staring at the warm turf fire. Meg refused to say more.

That night Ryan lay in bed. Every creak or sound from the old house made him jump. His body was covered in sweat, his hair was soaked, his right hand trembled in spasmodic motions. From outside came the sound of the howling Kerry coastal wind. On the window three loud raps announced that his visitation had begun. He got up out of bed and tried to switch on the bedroom light. Nothing happened. A white-blue glow came from under the bedroom door. Realizing that one way or another he would have to face its menace, he opened the door. Ahead, in the hallway at least seven foot tall stood a winged figure in black. Its face seemed to shimmer, one moment a bird, the next a wrinkled old woman. The image blinked two to three times and was gone. In its place stood the young girl of his dreams, dressed once again in her pale white dress. She beckoned with her finger. Crying with fear now Ryan walked unwillingly toward her. She didn't attack him, or scream, or do any of the things that Ryan expected. She just took him by the hand and led him outside, onto the moonlit beach.

She turned then and pointed back to where the summer house had been. Gone was the house, and in its place hovered what seemed like an old longship. The longship glowed and was, on closer inspection, coloured gold.

Then she turned him toward the sea. Night seemed like day now. He saw men who had travelled to Ireland in boats of leather and hide coming ashore. Among them a Druid who could calm the waves. She showed him the King's Palace at Tara, Maeve and her bulls, the coming of Patrick, and the white friars. She showed him the plundering Norsemen in their terrible fury – the men of iron who married the old stock. She showed him the nobles leaving Ireland's shores bound for Spain and France. She showed him the great hunger and wept as she once again saw her children scattered to the four corners of the globe. She showed him a fair city in flames and her children giving their lives before the firing squads. She squeezed his hand so much he thought it would break. With spittle running from her mouth and malevolence streaming from her grip, she showed him the present, a land decimated with greed – neighbour refusing to help neighbour, politicians selling their people both dead and living, for personal gain. Her vulnerable children left uneducated, a language in terminal decline, a land left desecrated. Her greatest anger she saved for last. Her sacred temples, long survivors of a foreign occupation, were now torn up for housing, her hidden treasures destroyed for roads leading nowhere. Her landscape defaced for the greed of men. This all flashed through Ryan's brain in seconds. He screamed in pain. She left go of his arm, her appearance flashed, blinked and changed. In front of him now stood the tall crow-like creature he had seen before. It grasped his temples and roared a terrible scream of pain and anger. Instantly Ryan saw the office in Dublin again, the firm of civil engineers he worked for. He saw the contract for the new toll motorway they had won. He saw the destruction the road would cause. The creature roared again, and he saw the faces of his colleagues dead, killed in terrible ways. He saw politicians choking on their own blood. A government in collapse. He saw a time of desperation. He saw a plague that spread throughout the land. People choking on their own blood. He saw children suffer and die. He saw the riots, he saw the death, the terrible catastrophe that was to come. And he knew, he knew, it would all come true.

The creature let go of Ryan. In front of him the little girl was standing, smiling now, content. "Tell them I'm coming," she said. Then she turned and walked away in the direction of the boulder on the edge of the tide.

A week later, in one of the best hotels in Dublin, the engineering firm of Deane and Co. civil engineers held its Christmas party. The staff had earned its reward. It had been a good year. The new motorway would be a giant feather in the cap of this rising star of the Celtic Tiger. The dinner was excellent, a lavish five-course affair with young rare lamb as the entrée. Dixie Dean, chairman of Dean and Co. stood to give his festive speech and to enumerate the year's satisfactory developments. He was a happy man. The government had just awarded Dean and Co. the contract for the latest toll motorway that would feed the infrastructure of Ireland's new economy. Of course, there had been difficulties along the way, not least the environmental assessment and the historical survey, but, and Dixie smiled as he reflected on this, it was amazing how people in high places could be "persuaded" to see the wisdom of such a scheme. All in all, with minimal outlay, it had been a good result. Dixie launched into his speech with a confident gleam in his eye; he sincerely wished all of his staff a very merry Christmas and a prosperous New Year. Then he began to speak about the importance and of the new motorway and the benefits it would bring to its users. Just as he was warming to the topic of the new Ireland, the doors to the dining room flung open. Into the room erupted a bedraggled, unwashed, emaciated male figure. He screamed at them, bawling at the top of his voice, "Stop the road!" He cried and ran from person to person, screaming, "stop the road!" Following behind were the hotel bouncers. They quickly grabbed hold of him. They pulled him upright, unmasking Ryan's distraught face.

Dixie was amazed. "Ryan? Ryan Costello is that you," asked Dixie. Indeed it was, and he was obviously high or mad or both. "Christ what's the matter with you?"

Ryan wailed, "It's all of you I'm here for. You must not go ahead with that road,"

Dixie laughed. "Why, Ryan?"

"Because she is coming."

Dixie was enjoying this, Ryan had always irritated him. "Who is coming?" asked Dixie, a gleam in his eye.

"The queen," said Ryan. "The queen of phantoms."

Some of his former colleagues began to laugh. They had filled up on the mulled wine earlier so they were in boisterous spirits. The laughter became loud and hysterical when the bouncers dragged Ryan away. One or two looked on nervously, but most laughed and laughed and laughed.

The hotel staff called the police. Ryan was arrested and taken to Bridewell Garda station where a psychiatrist was called in. Ryan continued to scream and wail for most of the night until a sedative brought him some blessed relief.

No one saw the little girl enter the service entrance of the hotel. The cooks had slipped out back for a quick smoke during a lull in the busy evening schedule. The girl was barefoot, her white dress short and ragged. Her features were drawn, and a yellow tinge coloured her skin. She was a frail creature, and seemed out of place in a plush hotel in those heady affluent times. No one saw the little girl slip into the kitchen where she skipped merrily up to a stainless steel counter. There, a large bowl of whipped cream had been prepared, it was destined to be served with the festive plum pudding for the folks at the Christmas party. Holding her head back, she hawked and spat a viscous glob. She stared into the cauldron awhile and then, taking her index finger, she dipped it into the mixture. Withdrawing her finger, she tasted it and smiled. Then, as quietly as she had come, she skipped merrily out the door, mournfully humming the ancient "Coventry Carol" as she went.

Ryan woke to the sound of the mid-morning news being broadcast over the police station radio. He listened to the morning headlines. "Fifteen people are dead and twelve more are in critical condition after an outbreak of food poisoning at the Merrymount Hotel in Dublin last night. State health inspectors are still investigating the outbreak. It is believed it may have spread to a number of other hotels across the city. In other news, the minister for the Environment, Mr. Padraig Daly, was last night killed in a freak road accident. The Minister's driver, who bizarrely was not injured in the crash, stated that he had swerved to avoid a child walking toward the car in the middle of the road."

Ryan stopped listening. He closed his eyes and tried not to cry. He tried to think of happier times, of Christmas in his past. He thought of carols and lights and he remembered church bells ringing in the Christmas morn. They were ringing again now. Ringing across Dublin. They were ringing through the Boyne valley over the Bog of Allen and into the rest of Ireland beyond. They rang with such splendour that everyone heard the call and every man, woman and child, raised his head to listen.

Then the church bells went silent. Not a sound was heard. In his jail cell Ryan heard faint skipping footsteps somewhere nearby. He turned over in his bunk and faced the shadow of his cell wall. He was too afraid to look. The skips came closer. He heard a muffled giggle and then felt a cold breath on the side of his head followed by a sharp whisper in his ear, "Tell them I'm coming."

Veil Thinner

It is hard to believe. After all these years the ghosts are still with me. I thought that I would heal, that I would forget and feel something new, and in time, something different would take its place. How wrong I have been! I think back to the days of my youth, when I decided to explore the mysteries of what lies beyond this world, to find some meaning to this existence. In my journey I found a friend, the best friend I ever had. He was a wonderful friend, a bright inquisitive young man, and we searched for answers together. Yet all we found was fear and death.

My friend was David Ash, a young American who had come to Ireland to study at University College Cork. We met on the first day of class, and our friendship was wonderful, a true meeting of minds. We connected on the deepest of levels, and in time, were inseparable. David excelled in everything he did. He was a true scholar and a fine athlete, one of the few Americans who ever made the college Rugby team. He was one of the most popular students at the college and was often found in the company of some girl or another. I, on the other hand, was often invisible in the shadow of his vitality. I was seen as a hanger on, often mocked by my peers for the affection in which I held David. College girls were never in my vicinity, and my slight frame meant I had little hope of ever making the college rugby team, even though I trained as hard as the rest.

David and I held similar convictions in our academic research. We agreed that the limit of science was, in this day and age, almost exhausted. We felt that there was a need to search for knowledge in other places. We sought out this deeper knowledge. We were interested in the Occult, the Esoteric, particularly, we were interested in Paganism. It is laughable when I look back at it. We thought we were Druids, practitioners of the ancient magic of Ireland, privy to the secret knowledge of the hollow hills and ancient woodland. But we were just two boys playing at magic, delving into a religion that had long been forgotten, a religion that was a dormant way of viewing the world, better left behind in the mist of time, rather than glimpsed again, by us. But delve we did, and I've regretted it ever since.

We knew of the old Gaelic myth that a veil existed between our world and the spirit world. We also knew of the belief that at special times of the year, the veil thinned, and that some of our ancient ancestors believed it possible to glimpse the spirit world. We had done our research. It indicated that almost every ancient culture believed in an alternate reality to the one in which we find ourselves in this life. David particularly mentioned the Aboriginal "Dream Time" as a parallel of the Gaelic Otherworld. He felt that both the "Dream Time" and the "Gaelic Otherworld" were representations of the other side of the same supernatural veil that shrouded our world. David believed that given certain conditions, certain altered states, we the living could glimpse the Otherworld. So we delved, we took workshops, met other like-minded people, travelled to sacred sites around the country, until the time came when we found what we were looking for on the side of a mountain in West Cork. Joe Kantz was an eccentric German hippy that a pagan friend of mine had sent us in search of to get hold of some psilocybin I can still hear the old hippy laughing at us.

"Druwids? Ya?" he asked. "You come to me looking for mushrooms to get high and you tell me you're Druwids?

"Yes," David replied, insulted by this silly old hippy's attitude. "We are trying to do something serious." His patience was at an end. It had been a painful process, a three hour drive in the country and a half a mile hike up a gravel path to a shack that reeked of body odour and cannabis.

He chuckled again. "Ha, serious."

"Look, if you don't want to sell us any mushrooms, then let us know who will, down here in hippy-land," I replied.

He fixed me with his watery eyes, the narcotic element of the previous joint still evident within him. "I'll go you von bettar," he said. "I have just refined ointment, for such purposes as you boys are looking for. I'll give it to you for, say, three hundred Euro?"

"Are you kidding," asked David, exasperated. Three hundred Euro for a jar of crap?"

"Sis is no crap," he replied. "I've spent months working on it. It's the real thing."

"Have you tried it," asked David. "Does it work?"

"Vell, I haven't tried it yet, but I was going to in the next few weeks," answered Joe.

David turned to me. "We are out of here Michael," he said. "Our German hippy friend here is full of it."

It was the only time in my life when I ever pleaded with him. I took him aside to the corner of the shack. "Give it a go, David," I said. "Look, I'll pay for it.

Remember that cute Pagan friend of mine? The one I've been chasing but can never get off with? Yeah? Well she says he is the real deal."

"He's conning us," said David. "How can you trust him?"

"Katie told me that he is the real thing," I repeated. "If it's good enough for her, then I'm willing to take the chance. Trust me on this?"

David was silent. He then put his finger to his lips and mused. "I guess we'll try it." And, so we bought the ointment off the ageing hippy and headed back to Cork.

In a way, it suited David. He had been talking about an ointment. He had read in depth on the use of henbane in medieval Europe. Henbane had caused hallucinations to the supposed "witches" who had rubbed it into their skin. Apparently, it gave the 'witch' in question hallucinations of flying. We hoped that this ointment would have the desired effect of lifting the veil and allowing us to travel at will on the other side.

David and I spent the next three weeks figuring out where the ritual site would be. Where the site was concerned, David wanted the woods. "Where better to get in touch with land spirits," he would argue. I wanted something more dangerous, edgy.

"Look," I said. "Let's use a graveyard."

But he was not to be swayed. "No, it's the other world in its entirety we want to spy upon, not just the dead. Besides, it would be wrong to ritual there, wouldn't it?

"I suppose it would," I agreed, disappointed.

In the end, we agreed to perform the ritual in a small grove of yew trees, near an isolated farmhouse a mile or so from my home. The grove was situated at the top corner of a meadow that ran steeply into a bog-stream at the bottom of a field. Two other fields bordered the grove from either side, which gave the grove a triangular appearance when viewed from the hill above.

On a warm spring evening, we set off across the fields with everything we needed for our ritual stored in a backpack. David was happy. He whistled as our feet trampled on the fresh spring grass of the field, leaving a trail in our wake. When we arrived at the grove, we cleared a large circle of ground within the cluster of trees. He smiled at me, excited, a look of enchantment in his eyes. This was our night, and it was time to get everything ready. Night began to fall. We gathered a mound of kindling timber within the grove and cleared fallen debris in preparation for our circle. Soon, a roaring camp fire reflected on the canopy over head. The fire's red glow mingled with the green leaves above. A gentle breeze above swayed the leaves. The effect was a colourful rustling of light that shimmered throughout the grove. It seemed as if the Iron Age were alive again and that we truly were Druids in a sacred grove. We gazed at each other, my affection for him growing by the hour. Here was a true pioneer, a true seeker of knowledge and I, I was only a minion caught in his wake.

With a gentle nod of his head, he let me know that it was time to begin. We had prepared for this. We had fasted, bathed, meditated. It was time. We undressed quickly, the fire warming our bare skin. David opened the odd shaped vial and rubbed the ointment all over. When he was finished, I did the same. We lay for on the ground for a long time, working on a light meditation, preparing ourselves one final time. Eventually, David rose and took a brand from the fire. He walked in a clockwise direction around the edge of the circle and spoke in old Irish these words:

"I dedicate this circle to ancestors, to the ones who walked before us on this island beloved of the Mother Goddess. Spirits of old, consecrate this sacred circle, and walk within. Be with us, as we wish to be with you."

We followed with a deep intonation of the Gaelic "Imbas" or "inspiration." "Imbas" is the creative spirit that Druids believe runs through all things. It is the source of Druid power. David led in a low baritone hollow sound that reverberated around the grove.

"IIIIIMMMMMMBAAAASSSS."

I responded in kind, "IIIIMMMMMBAAASSSS," and together we finished the call to the sacred spirit.

"IIIIMMMMMBAAASSSSS."

We sat again on our rugs. Night had fallen, and within the glade the firelight cast furtive shadows about the grove. A quarter moon lit the night sky, and we waited.

It started with a rising feeling of anxiety within us both. Though the fire was hot and the night mild, we shivered with a sense of fright and cold combined. David began to tremble.

"Michael, I'm afraid. What have we done?" he asked.

I also felt a rising panic stir within my chest. I had the urge to get away but when I tried to move, my body didn't respond.

"It'll be all right. Stay with it," I responded. "I'm here for you."

He let out a violent scream, the grove reverberating with the sound of his fright. He called and called for help. My voice failed me. My head fell back against the rug and I lay there unmoving, my eyes stretched wide in the psychedelic voyage that I had entered, and within the grove, I began to see.

Rings of light exploded and contracted. The exploding rings were surrounded by white shapes that grew and diminished, only to grow back again within seconds. Beyond the distinguishable glow of the fire lay a mist, twisted grey shapes coiling and moving within it. The terrible sound of crying rose over the grove, a sound so sad that it could break a thousand hearts. The exploding colours changed again. Deeper now, these navy and purples shot to and fro within the grove. The keening stopped and was replaced by a guttural animal-like sound, a harsh growling. I was beside myself with fright. Tears ran from my eyes, and yet they were still locked open in that same psychedelic stare. Who knows how long the colours and the sounds went on for? We lost all sense of time, all sense of ourselves, and we drifted for some time on the other side of the veil. I remember angry voices, telling me to come back, to return to the glade, to take care of my friend. At some point I regained a semblance of consciousness and looked over at David. He was sitting up, his head moving clock-wise, staring, and his eyes wide in fright. When I turned to see what he stared at, I saw what we had come to see. Ringing the grove were hosts of faces, hundreds of pale yellow faces, that glared upon us, some malevolent, some inquisitive and some simply laughing at us. I was caught in the grip of their glare. Their eyes burrowed accusations into me. They were angry at me.

From behind the crowd of faces came the sound of trotting hooves. The crowd parted, and a large white form entered the grove. I couldn't look. I buried my face into my hands and turned over to face the ground. I heard David scream again and again and again. I lost myself then, lost all feeling, all consciousness and I swooned for a time in oblivion.

When I woke, it was morning. The fire had burned out and I could hardly move from the chill of sleeping in the open air. David was in a terrible state. He couldn't get up, he was in such pain. I hoisted myself up and tried to help, but he couldn't move. It was then that I ran for help.

Later, in the hospital, I stared on his swollen face which still held traces of his angelic features. For hours, I sat by this gentle man and gazed at him. The hours became days and the days, weeks. It took David three months to recover and in that time, we grew apart. I had found a girlfriend by then. Samantha, a wonderful little country girl who was interested in witchcraft. In the following months after his release from hospital, David withdrew from college life. He stopped attending lectures and refused to socialize with me.

It was in early May of the following year that David called me to his room. He was dishevelled. He hadn't washed in days. But what was worse was that his face was bruised.

"Have you been in a fight," I asked.

"In a manner of speaking," he replied. "I've taken to fighting things I cannot see. Angry voices that beat me at night, they tell me that I am to join them soon. They tell me I've seen too much. What do you think, Michael. Have I seen too much?" he asked, his voice tormented. "What haunts me? That grove? Those faces we saw? Is there something I should know," he pleaded with me.

I shrugged my shoulders. "You picked the site, my friend," I replied.

He nodded forlornly. "I did," he said in a resigned voice. "Go home, Michael. You may not see me again."

"Nonsense!" I answered in shock. "You'll be right as rain. Come stay with Samantha and me."

But he would not. He simply ushered me to the door and whispered, "Let me be. Perhaps tonight I shall see all."

That was the last I ever saw of David Nash. Later that night, on hearing David screaming, his landlady called the police. After breaking down the door, they found him battered and bleeding and dead in a corner of his room. The landlady swore that no one had entered his room that night. And the police had found the door locked on arrival. The autopsy revealed that David had died from trauma to the chest and head as a result of being beaten. The strange thing was that the coroner had found hoof prints on his chest and his back. The marks were consistent with being trampled by a large animal. When analysed, they were found to be the hoof prints of a large goat. It was a perplexing case.

To this day David's face remains with me. In my mind's eye I see him, the athletic young intellectual. He was the most popular student on campus. I still see him: the beautiful man that he was and the wasted corpse he became. I suppose, I should have told him that Joe Kantz had been involved in a weird cult in the seventies. A cult where a young teenage member had committed suicide. But it didn't seem to matter at the time. David wanted to be a Druid after all, he wanted his ointment. Who was I to stop him?

Our ritual site was located on top of an old famine pit, a mass grave where the dead were buried when the graveyards overflowed during the Great Hunger. I could have mentioned that to him as well. After all, I'd grown up not much more than a mile from the grove. But David wanted to see the other side. Who was I to deny my friend? The best friend I ever had! And, why shouldn't I have used less of the ointment on my skin? Joe had warned me not to use too much, so I took his advice. I had to protect myself, didn't I? I had to make sure I was there for David when he came back from his journey on the other side of the veil. It's just so sad that he died so young and full of life.

Mahain's Grave

Everything felt different. Though I had viewed these sights many times in youth, now, after so many years, the winding lane and sloping hill that led up to Currabinny Wood were strange. A fog shrouded my progress, and in the distance the lighthouse of Roche's Point bellowed a low-pitched warning to passing ships at sea. Though the weather was mild, the rhythmic pulse of the Atlantic lapped loudly against the shoreline beyond.

Turning the final bend of the lonely road, I caught the first glimpse of green among the tall branches of oak, ash, and beech beyond. The fog clung to the trees in swirling wisps that rose and fell with each summer gust of Atlantic breeze It was the time of Lughnasadh, when my ancestors had practised their ancient beliefs on this craggy outpost where earth, sea, and sky combined.

My professor, like me a native of this area, had held the belief that here Druids once practised their pagan ways, long after Patrick had converted the Gael to the message of the Nazarene. The kindly old man had told me of the writings of Brother Mahain, an ancient monk, whom he believed had been pagan and who now lay buried in secret in the neolithic tumulus at the top of the wood. He had expressed a wish to one day return and seek the grave of Mahain at Currabinny.

I had spent long years pouring through Ireland's early manuscripts. Much writing had been lost, but traces of Mahain remained and these pointed to his burial on the hilltop. My research had also led me to another conclusion that within Mahain's grave lay buried an "ancient secret."

My professor questioned me, but, in the end, dismissed my theory. When pressed, he mentioned that he had heard of this before, but he and scholars like him had rejected the theory. Now, I trod on, in search of what many believed could never be found.

The locals called the tumulus "The Giant's Grave," – a bare collection of moss-covered Neolithic stones at the summit of the wood, a resting place for a giant of ancient folklore. What an ignorant shower the locals were – to be a giant in ancient times was merely to be tall, and the manuscripts I consulted had alluded to Mahain's height.

Locals – these were the people I had grown up with in this parish, the offspring of hovel cottage dwellers and drunken royal navy sailors stationed at the base in nearby Haulbowline. A common, degenerate horde, whose only joy it seemed was to make the owners of the nearby sheebeens richer and themselves and their children poorer. I was glad that I had moved abroad so many years before to study at Miskatonic University in New England.

Somehow a few of the older locals had heard of my plan and had visited my lodging last night. They spoke of disturbing what should not be disturbed and of letting the past go, for what was gone must be let go, for the good of all. But I had greater things on my mind than folk tales.

I entered the wood under a darkening sky. I'd known this outcrop of woodland since I was a boy. Here my family had gathered for picnic lunches, never knowing what treasures lay below. Through the fog that now shadowed the forest path and under the dark green canopy, I ventured further.

Within, the wood was oppressive and humid; the sweat that clung to me would grow cold when the evening waned. Mine was not the widened carriage path laid down for a long-forgotten gentry, my path was a narrow, serpentine, mud-covered lane whose putrid detritus made a sickly squelch under my boots. Black roots of ash and oak protruded from the path, coiling and clasping at my feet, like the grotesque tentacles of some underground creature come to take its prey back to some hidden depths below the wood. I passed sick, moss-covered trees whose trunks and branches were twisted and gnarled, whose bark had in places rotted away to reveal the dying wood beneath.

I smiled, envisioning the harvest I would reap. I would, if my research proved correct, make a discovery that would change all known perceptions of "The Druids." I would uncover their ancient secrets and live the life I had planned for years. I could see it, the books, the lecture circuit, and the TV interviews. It was all so very close.

"Of course, the Druids left no written legacy," I could hear myself telling the TV host. "But this artefact is conclusive proof that not all the Irish converted to Christianity en mass, so to speak." Oh, yes my discovery would change things, that was for sure.

The path turned uphill. I left behind the muddy, root-infested slime for gravel-covered ground that crunched underfoot, and the forest canopy no longer blotted out the sky. I reached the summit and came upon a grassy clearing, circular in shape, ringed by species of trees old and new. Of all the species present, the oak was absent. At the centre of the clearing lay the ancient stones, the grave of Mahain.

Night was nearing. I unpacked my shovel and compass and got to work. I had read in the book of Lecan that this wood had been a Neolithic cemetery, a place of burial for the ancients and, of course, for Mahain himself. It would be a slow dig. The sweat poured from my forehead as I drove the spade into the ancient soil. With each passing load the sky grew darker. In time, I took the camper light from my rucksack and, in almost total darkness, continued working.

Surely it was here! The manuscripts had mentioned it, some tableau of gold that the ancients had made pilgrimages to see on this isolated hill. I dug with a frenzy that I had never known before, my shovel making soft cutting noises as it sliced into the earth of the tumulus. Over and over again I threw my body into this act of discovery. Finally I heard a faint crunching, I bent down with my flashlight to look. There lay the long dead collection of sea shells -the midden- for which Neolithic remains in Ireland were noted. I was getting closer.

Above, a harvest moon shone through the canopy and illuminated my work with a pale glow. I saw that I had left a crater-like hole in the mound's side. Night time noises filled the wood now. Little creatures shuffled in the undergrowth to my left. Night birds flew through the branches above. A whistle of summer wind caught the heavy limbs and made them sway. I continued to dig.

A strange light glowed pale among the trees, bobbling and bouncing. Its glow coated the wood in an atmosphere of fear. The light seemed to move in a circular fashion until it eventually was eclipsed by the density of forest. Something was here in Currabinny and about to disturb my work.

I stopped what I was doing and took a few steps to the edge of the clearing. I was rewarded for my inquiry when suddenly the light reappeared and I caught a glimpse of a white form holding what seemed an old fashioned lantern.

Unafraid, I followed this light, this spirit or wraith, whatever it was, along its pathway through the wood. Branches scratched my face. A strange whispering filled the wood. I thought I glimpsed in the velvet darkness a pair of yellow eyes. I was sure now that some spirit, some revenant, was abroad and set upon disrupting my find.

I have no recollection of how long I followed. In time, my legs ached and I stopped, sweat scalding my cheeks and stung my eyes. My hands were bruised and cut from the broken foliage. Yet through the moonlit trees, I spied a tall figure walking with purpose along a narrow path close to my left. A white glow seemed to surround the form in the distance. It was a tall, cloaked figure, its hair braided in the Celtic manner of old. Mahain was alive! Through some lost Druid knowledge, he walked these forest paths still!

The creature – Mahain – knew the forest, for soon he led me back onto the sloping path to the grave. I followed at a distance. I saw him examine my work and watched him note every detail of what he must have thought was the damage to his tomb. For a while he stood surveying the monument, then he knelt. To do what, I could not see.

What was he? A vampire that could leave his grave and walk among the living at night? Some ancient ghost that projected the image it had held in life? Whatever this creature was, he stood between me and the prize I had so long striven for. I made my decision then. I crept softly towards the unsuspecting ghoul of old, holding my shovel tight. I crossed the grassy clearing in silence, making gentle footfalls as I went. The shovel's edge sparkled silver in the moonlight. Within two feet of him, I raised the shovel above my head.

I must have made some noise, some sound inconsistent with the night sounds of this creature's home, for Mahain turned, raised his head and let out a strange cry.

With all my strength, I brought the edge of the blade down on his neck. A wet sickening thud filled the clearing. A gush of blood spurted from the creature's neck, his head bounced gently to earth on one side of the tomb and rolled off into the brambles beyond…

I stooped to look for my prize. But then a worry nagged me. Where was this head? Where was the proof that Mahain would never again walk this forest. I searched about where I had dug, and even the entire clearing beyond. Fear coursed through me. Could ghoul of old rise from his death and replace his head on his very shoulders? I searched the brambles, growing more agitated as the moon waned. Panic seized me. I ran from Currabinny as fast as the night wind would take me and returned to my lodgings.

Oh, how I tossed and turned that night – such dreams! I dreamt of pagan dances in a fire-lit glade, of ancient tomb builders on a rocky outcrop, of a carriage jaunt with Victorian ladies whose faces grew rotten when I gazed upon them. I soared in my dreams above the hills of Currabinny. Below, every tree top held the head of Mahain. A forest of severed heads laughed at me as I passed – a terrible evil laughter, echoing in the surrounding hills, a perverse derision directed at me. I dreamt I floated upon the ocean with Mahain's headless corpse until we drifted to the shores of Currabinny, and on reaching the land the headed treetops whispered again and again, "You have my head but I have the knowledge for eternity now." The creature's corpse beat its fist upon the shore, a reverberation that echoed in my ears. Again and again the carcass beat its fist upon the shore until I woke to the sound of knocking at my bedroom door.

"Mr. Greening? Open up, please it's the police."

They wanted to search my room. For what, they would not say. Why would I stop them? They who would never know the importance of my work or the sights I had seen in my dreams, they who never knew who Mahain was and how I had ended his evil presence in the quaint little wood. You can imagine my shock upon their opening my suitcase and exposing a plastic bag within. But, reader, can you imagine my screams when, on pulling forth the bag's grisly contents they drew forth not the head of that demon Mahain but instead the wounded head and agonized face of my old college professor!

They put me in handcuffs and brought me here to St. Anne's Hospital, a pleasant Victorian building overlooking the river Lee. Time has passed since that faithful night. How long, I cannot say. I have heard my doctors mention something about psychosis. I spend my days in this tiny cell until I can return again to Currabinny. But at night I soar above the hills and valleys of home once more. I soar on the winds of my dreams ever searching, but never finding, that lost ancient knowledge that can only be found deep within the grave of Mahain.

The Samhain Party

The light fades. From the small window in our cloister, I look across the Blackwater valley. The sun is setting over our ravaged land. I remember the glowing emerald green of our island, once famous for its holy places and ancient ruins. But that land is no more. Tonight I look upon a barren landscape, made bleak with ice and snow. The evening sun turns the sky a kaleidoscope of pink against the encroaching dark. November eve – tonight the veil between this world and the next will fade and vanish. The dead will walk among us once again. I wait in my freezing cell, my chin shivering. My vision dims, and I remember a time before the chastisement, a time of affluence, of unbelief. Most of all, I remember a man named Chris Stout.

Chris Stout was a product of another time, a child of the Celtic Tiger. A twenty-five-year-old software developer, he was overpaid and over-opinionated. He had little time in his life for anything other than the materialistic. When questioned about the spiritual, he championed the atheist cause. He rebuked the notion of an almighty spiritual being. He poured scorn on the idea of any kind of life after the one that we live, and he always finished his atheistic sermons with an urging to the unfortunate subject to be as ruthless as possible in this life. Because, he suggested, what really mattered was "how much" rather than anything else. It was with scorn that Chris accepted an invitation from a friend to attend a Pagan gathering at Halloween, or Samhain, as the believers in the "Old Gods" choose to call the celebration. The friend was a Pagan who held Samhain to be one of the year's major religious celebrations. The gathering, in the form of a ritual, was to be followed by a feast. Chris was assured there would be plenty of wine. Chris, who never missed an opportunity for free alcohol, agreed to attend.

The gathering was held in the northern part of County Cork, not far from the town of Mallow. Chris arrived late, having stayed an extra hour to work on a project he had been developing for his employer. Stephen, the friend who had invited Chris to the gathering, introduced him to the twenty or so other participants.

Never a lad to be shy in a social situation, Chris struck up a conversation with a thirty-something blonde.

He used his usual palaver of being a successful IT professional to charm her. The woman, however, seemed unimpressed. She kept changing the subject back to the evening at hand. This was a "special night," she said, their one night of the year, and all things were possible on this night. Chris, not really in tune with this line of reasoning moved on.

He spotted a pretty brunette nibbling a piece of Barmbrack across the room and decided to try his luck there. He greeted the girl with his usual confidence, and she responded in a friendly enough way. Forewarned from his last conversation, Chris let the woman do the talking. Again the subject was of Samhain, this hallowed evening. Chris, his curiosity piqued, delved deeper. He asked the girl what was Samhain, why was it a special night?

She giggled and replied, "Because it is on this night that all beings from the 'Otherworld' are granted leave to return to earth. It is the carnival time of spirits. On this night that the Sidhe are abroad."

"And who are the Sidhe," asked Chris, an incredulous tone in his voice.

A man's voice, powerful and strong, answered from behind. "They are the old folk, a race of supernatural beings, one of the original settlers of Ireland."

Chris turned to see a tall man, broad shouldered, his grey hair braided, dressed in a hooded white robe.

The man continued, "They were called the Tuatha De Danann. When the first human tribes known as the Milesians came to this island, they found the Tuatha De Danann. The Milesians knew they would never conquer the De Danann, so they made an agreement. The Tuatha De Danann were given rule over the realms underground, while the Milesians kept the overground realm. The De Danann from that time on inhabited the underworld; we find them at such gateways to the underworld as raths, burial mounds or barrows. They are now the "Sidhe" or fairy folk, and are granted leave to return to earth for one night of the year. This night was and still is Samhain."

Chris looked around the cottage. All the people at the feast had stopped to pay attention. The man seemed to be held in some kind of awe. Chris said nothing, only nodded. To him, the story was laughable – underground fairies, what a joke. This guy had eaten too many mushrooms.

"You must be Chris," said the man. "Stephen mentioned you'd be visiting our gathering. Welcome and blessed be. I am Avon, head witch for tonight's circle."

Chris smiled and shook the man's hand. "Glad to meet you, Avon," said Chris, trying not to laugh at the seriousness with which the man took himself.

"Stephen tells me you are an unbeliever?"

"That's right," said Chris. "I'm just here for the feast; I'm not really a spiritual person."

"I don't believe that," said Avon. "The fact that you are here at all shows you have some interest or curiosity in what we do here."

"I don't think so," said Chris. "I just like a good party."

"Don't be so sure," Avon replied. "Spirituality often chooses a person rather than they choose it. Especially on Samhain, of all nights." Join us outside for our circle."

"I think I'll stay here in the house, said Chris."

"No, come join us," said the brunette, slipping her arm around Chris's shoulder. Chris, not needing to be asked twice, caught the girl's hand and allowed her to lead him out into the adjoining field, where a pile of timber was laid, ready to be lit.

Avon joined the group. As the fire was being lit, the group joined hands and the incantations began. Chris was trying not to laugh at most of what was being said. Soon the fire blazed and a metal chalice containing mead was passed around. Chris began to lose his control over his laughter as some of the group undressed and began to prostrate themselves before the fire. When Avon held his hands aloft and called on the ancestors to visit the fire. it was too much. Chris burst out laughing. The group stopped and stared. All at once he felt surrounded, caught in the malevolent glances of the group. Chris's stomach went hollow. The colour drained from his face, and he felt a foreboding as if something had been broken and couldn't be fixed. Avon, a dark rage of fury masked over his face, glared.

Holding his hands aloft, he again called on the spirits, asking them "To guide those who are lost, while teaching those who pour scorn on others, of their powerful existence."

It was Chris's turn to grow angry now. Who was this guy to use his little bit of power to frighten anyone? Forgetting the brunette whose hand he was holding, he broke from the circle and made his way back to the house. The remaining revellers who had not joined the circle asked Chris what was wrong. Over a few stiff brandies, Chris relayed that he hadn't been made welcome at the fire. This astonished the revellers. Wasn't everyone always welcome at Avon's circle? Then the gatherers returned from the fire. Chris attempted to lose himself in the crowd, chatting cordially and moving from group to group. For the next hour or so he managed to do this. But he couldn't help feeling that he was being watched, and many times during the remainder of the gathering he turned to see who was watching him. He saw nobody. At one o'clock the gathering broke up. Chris asked his one friend if he wanted a lift home.

"After the way you've behaved tonight," replied Stephen, "I don't think so."

Chris shrugged his shoulders and left. Outside, a clear night sky sparkled with billions of stars in the cold night air. Chris shivered and opened the door to his car.

"Just because you don't see or touch something, doesn't mean that it's not there." Avon spoke from behind Chris in the driveway.

"Oh, come on, Avon," said Chris. "We are not talking physical science here. We are talking about folklore, make believe, right up there with Santa Claus."

"Don't be so sure," replied Avon. "These beliefs, while they may be folklore today, were once sacred customs."

"Well, whatever substance is in the old Hocus Pocus you believe in, it's long, long dead," said Chris.

"That may well be," replied Avon. "But be sure you are careful driving home tonight. Should you stray off the beaten track, you may find that the old ones are not as dead as you believe!"

Chris snickered, started up the engine, and left Avon behind in a shower of gravel. He began the long journey home. Miles of country lanes lay before him. He slipped his Pink Floyd CD into the car stereo. But the CD wouldn't play. Neither would the radio work. Odd, he thought, since there was power going to the stereo. He turned off the stereo and continued driving. The road was narrow; a canopy of trees created a tunnel overhead, giving Chris a claustrophobic feeling. Chris caught the glare of headlights further up the road and dimmed his lights. He noticed almost immediately that he wasn't getting any closer to the lights. This started to trouble him, and he felt a strange tingling in his neck.

He came to a bend in the road, where the road led over a bridge. When he got to the other side of the bridge, the lights disappeared. Ahead of him large potholes cratered the road. Gravel was strewn all over its surface, and a faint drizzle an hour before had made the road greasy. Chris drove on, the car bumping and jumping in and out of the potholes. Foolishly he didn't slow down; rather, without realizing it, he increased his speed. His concentration centred on the now-stationary light that had reappeared. His focus remained steady, and Chris began to drift within his mind. The car was really taking a hammering, yet still its speed increased. Chris was now lost in some sort of dream, unaware of the road. The reality of his situation suddenly dawned on Chris, but it was too late. The car spun out of control, broke the verge of the road, and careered down a steep embankment heavily overgrown with saplings and gorse.

The fall seemed to never stop; the loud bangs and crashes jolted Chris in his driver's seat. The windscreen shattered and its contents spattered over Chris, cutting into his cheek and forehead. The car hit an old oak at the bottom of the incline. Chris, not wearing any seat belt, was knocked unconscious when his head smashed into steering wheel.

Ten minutes later he woke, his head pounding. He tried to move and instantly regretted it. Every fibre was a roaring sea of pain. Gingerly he felt his nose; it seemed twisted, obviously broken when his head struck the steering wheel. He discovered that his shirt was soaking wet and then a realization struck him. His shirt was soaked with blood. Once more, he tried to move, but again the pain ripped through him. His feet were trapped in a tangled mass of metal where the pedals used to be. He tried with all his strength to move one leg but the pain was excruciating, and he still couldn't release his leg. He looked around and realized what a state the car was in. The entire passenger side pillar was smashed. The front bonnet was folded up from the impact as well. He was trapped inside.

Chris wondered how long it would be before anyone would come to his help when a loud rustling from the bushes to his left made him jump. His reaction caused him to twist his leg, and blinding pain swept through him again. A wall of black rose up to meet Chris as he passed out.

A sharp tapping on the driver side window brought Chris back from the darkness. Slowly he opened his eyes again. His body was still trapped in the ruins of the vehicle, but the pain had eased. Again the tapping on Chris's window sounded. He didn't want to look. He wanted to curl up and sleep away from this valley, away from Samhain and its dark mysteries. The tapping continued. Chris glanced at the window. Through the darkness, he made out a small hand. He looked more closely and a woman's shape melted into view from the darkness. Then he heard a voice from the shape.

"Open the window, child."

"No," answered Chris. "Who are you? What do you want?"

"I am the voice of this isle," returned the shape. "I am the past, the present, and the future. I am the Flower

Maiden in May and the Hag in winter. Open the window, child, for I am here to help you."

"No!" screamed Chris, thinking "I'm hallucinating. This isn't real."

The woman peered in. Seeing her features for the first time, Chris thought he would go insane. In the window of the car was the most hideous, most deformed woman he had ever seen.

She smiled her toothless grin, "Behold my true form this night, little creature. Tonight I am the Hag of Giamos, and should you scorn my help on this night, then there are others abroad who will teach you."

Her wizened hands grabbed at his neck, sharp bony fingers sinking into his flesh. Chris couldn't breathe. He cast a look at the terrible face again. It was smiling.

When Chris woke, he felt his neck and found no pain there. Still he was trapped in the car. But the Hag was nowhere to be seen. He checked for his mobile phone, but he remembered it was in the glove compartment, now ruined from the crash. He wondered at the strange hallucination he'd just had. In the distant hills a dog howled and was answered with another call, closer by. Chris shivered. Outside the car the darkness was total, a velvet wall of black that encircled the car. Suddenly a pinprick of orange light appeared, then it seemed to grow larger in the darkness. Chris' spirits soared; at last someone from the party, or maybe a neighbour, had come to rescue him. The light gradually grew larger. Eventually, Chris made out the shape of a large man carrying a lantern. Chris cried out for help. His happiness at being found was overcoming the pain now beginning to return. The figure approached.

"Help me!" cried Chris. "I've been hurt."

"Are you lost?" came the voice from the figure, not five feet from the car.

Chris still couldn't make out the man's features. "I just need some help," said Chris. "Please can you call an ambulance?"

"I'm sorry, my friend," said the figure. "I can help only those who are lost. If you tell me you are lost, I'll be sure and see you right." As he spoke, the figure came into Chris's view for the first time. Chris beheld a man in old-fashioned clothes like those worn by people in the famine. Where the man's face should have been was the outline of a skull.

"For my name is Jack, Jack O'Lantern, and I help all who are lost on this night," said the figure, now reaching for the door handle. Just when Chris was about to scream, a crescendo of howling began not far off to the right. The dogs that had howled earlier were now baying a terrible sound. The figure turned to look behind him.

"Unlucky for you boy, it seems Donn and his hounds have come. Better to be away, out of sight, when the Soul Stealer comes." The figure retreated in to the darkness, and slowly the lantern faded away. Chris was alone again.

Chris waited, trembling. The howling of the dogs grew louder. Closer and closer the howling came until the noise was deafening. Crying from fright by now, he repeated to himself that this was not happening. Outside the car the howling died down and Chris heard the trotting of feet. He heard the first cracking of timber in the woods beyond and shivered uncontrollably when a pack of hounds came into view: strange light-coloured hounds with dark ears and fire-red eyes. Hot tears scalded his cheeks. More cracking and breaking of timber sounded from the woods beyond. A ferocious guttural roar filled the clearing, a sound that seemed to make the very ground shake. A green glow moved from the direction of the sounds in the wood. Slowly the glow shrouded the clearing where Chris lay trapped. Through the glow he could make out branches and foliage being decimated where something large, moving very fast, was racing through the woods. Closer and closer it came, until the final branch snapped and into the clearing ran what

Chris thought was the devil himself. Halting before the vehicle was a huge horned creature with a body that glowed crimson. The howling of hounds started up again, building quickly until it reached an unearthly crescendo. Outstretched in his hands the creature held a great whip, which snaked out and lashed the hounds furiously. Then the noise receded and the creature approached.

Chris turned his gaze toward it, a monstrous figure at least eight feet tall, its head, the shape of a bull, with bull's horns each a foot wide. Its face was human but its eyes glowed an eerie green. From its fanged mouth arose a hideous cackle.

Then the creature spoke. "Pitiful wretch, your fate is to die alone in this darkness. Tonight your soul will scream its fiery fate in Anuinn, the place of torment."

A huge taloned hand reached through the open window, grabbed his shoulder, and wrenched his torn body from the car. Chris couldn't think any more. His screams became childish whimpers. Talons tore into his flesh, and Chris was lifted off his feet. Up they rose, impossibly up, above the clearing and into the star-speckled sky. Farther and farther until Chris couldn't breathe. His consciousness began to swim.

In the blur of his vision he saw the Samhain party and all that had happened that night. He heard Avon's voice saying that spirituality often chooses the person rather than he chose it. He whimpered again when he realized that he had indeed been chosen. The taloned arm snaked out and struck Chris hard, snapping his head backward and dulling his consciousness. The creature screamed into his face. Through swirling vision and the green eyes of the face in front of him, Chris saw the brunette. He heard her voice, saying that this was Samhain and on Samhain anything was possible. A realization hit Chris then: this was a magical night. Anything was possible. He didn't have to die tonight, he could at least try to save himself. He could at least believe he could fight back. Perhaps belief was enough, belief was all he had, belief that if he fought, he might somehow survive this. He flailed his arms, throwing punches with all his strength. The creature screamed its anger, but Chris roared back his new-found defiance and kept on punching and kicking. The creature roared again, but seemed to loosen his grasp. Heartened, Chris kept fighting. Mustering the last of the strength he had left, he gave the creature a heavy push and broke the demon's grasp. Then he was falling through the blackness. Over and over his body turned in a fall that seemed to never end.

When Chris awoke, he was shocked to find two Gardaí restraining him. The police had been called to an early-morning report of a car skidding off the road at Blaney's Curve. They'd found the car in perfect order on the verge of the road and had assumed the driver was asleep when they attempted to wake him. In his confusion, Chris had struggled. On seeing that the clearing in which the car had landed was gone and that he was on the verge of the Mallow road, he stopped resisting immediately. At the Mallow Garda station he was questioned Not wishing to add to his predicament, Chris told the Gardaí that he had fallen asleep when driving and must have skidded off the road. As for his resistance upon being woken, he apologized for his display and said he had gotten a fright. Garda Dorgan had been suspicious and continued to question Chris, but he answered all the queries well and was released with a caution.

A period of soul searching followed for Chris Stout, a search that yielded no answers. In time he quit his job and rented a cottage in the mountains of West Cork. But even after escaping to the wilds, his torment continued. He spent his days pondering what exactly had happened that Samhain night. His nights were full of terrors and dreams of the old "hag" who had visited him. His family and friends worried for a while, but within six months they took his decision to live in the country to be permanent. After that, their own pursuits took over and they worried no more. Life was busy in those heady times. They left him behind in the mountains to whatever fate they thought he'd chosen

Chris became a man in a perpetual spiritual crisis. That is when he visited me. Here at Mourne Abbey, he told me his tale. Having travelled far on this earth and seen many strange things, I was not incredulous of his story. But what could I do? I had very little comfort to give to his immediate fears. After a number of such visits, I heard his confession and absolved Chris from any sins he may have committed. He returned to his cottage, where he lives to this day. As the seasons passed he became more reclusive. Eventually, I saw Chris Stout no more.

The evening sky is now black. The dead are among us again on this holy evening. Against the window of my cell I light a single candle to guide the blessed ancestors home. I hope they can still recognize their mortal homes, for Ireland has changed so much. I hope they are not still angry with us. My eyes grow moist and I shed tears again. For this land, for its people, and for all the other Chris Stouts who didn't listen.

The Session

"Mark! I'm glad I caught you before you left. I see you have packed most of your things. Would you like a hand with that box?"

"No thanks, Mike, I can manage."

"Thirty years in the job, a good pension, and a fine retirement ahead of you. To be honest I wouldn't mind going with you! You must be delighted, eh?

"Yeah, I suppose I am."

"You don't seem overly enthusiastic, Mark. You were in great form at the dinner last night. Is anything wrong?"

"Oh, just something I found in my old desk, a session tape that I hadn't seen in ages. It reminded me of a difficult case I dealt with in the eighties."

"It's unlike you to let the job bother you like that, especially today of all days. But look, Mark, we all have troubling cases, that's the game we're in. Besides, it's over for you now, time to move on. Time to leave St. Margaret's behind. The future awaits!"

"That's the thing," said Mark. "This one has always been at the back of my mind, and now that I've found the tape, I'm perseverating on it. To be honest, it's been bothering me all day. I just wonder if I could have done more for that kid."

"Listen, Mark, you are a great psychologist. You know it and we all know it. Enjoy your retirement, you've earned it."

"Have I, Mike? Have I really done the best I could?"

"What is all this? No! Don't sit down and beat yourself up. Last night you were on top of the world, now look at you, sitting in that chair with your head in your hands. I won't have it. Give me that tape and I'll bin it."

"No," said Mark. "Listen to it first. Here, take the file and the tape and call me later. Tell me if I could have done anything more for that young kid. Take it home and listen to it, Mike."

"OK, OK, I will. Just go home now. Get some rest. You might have drunk too much last night. Go home, go to bed. I'll call later."

"He was only in his twenties, Mike. He'd grown up in Ireland, came over here for college. Poor kid, poor, poor kid."

"OK, Mark, I'll listen to it, now you go home!"

Session Tape 05
Subject: Clive Sullivan
Date: June 21 1985
Attending: Dr. Mark Webber

"Tell me, Clive, why graveyards? Why death and all its trappings?"

"Dr. Mark, aren't you supposed to be the therapist?"

"Yes, but psychotherapy begins and ends with the patient. We help you bring out what is inside. The answers are all within you, Clive. I don't have a magic wand. I can't just wave all your problems away."

"We have been here forever, and you have no answers, no diagnosis! We've been over this ground, I'm tired of this hospital, the same grotty rooms, the same crap food, and I'm sick of answering the same questions. I told you, I don't know why I was obsessed with death. I don't know why I went to funerals of people I didn't know. I don't know why I sat at the back of wakes and watched grieving families. I just don't know.

"Damn! This is annoying! But I will tell you something I do know, I know that when I walked in graveyards, among the dead, I felt comforted. I was at peace. I grew dependent on that peace. I still miss it. I have panic attacks when I don't feel it. Hell, it's why I'm here. Anxiety, right?"

"That's true, you were admitted with severe panic attacks, but they have eased off now. I think your psychotherapy is working. Stick at it, Clive."

"Errah stick at what? I feel like a dog chasing its tail. We've tried drugs, we've tried talking, what now, shock therapy?"

"That's a bit extreme, don't you think?"

"What's extreme, Doc? My anxiety? My acting out? Or maybe the fact that every night, I dream of being alone in a rain-swept graveyard in Ireland."

"Let's go over that one more time Clive, describe it again, what do you see?"

"Christ! This is tiresome!"

"Come on, Clive. Give it a go."

"All right, let me take a breath, and I'll try one last time."

"Go on, Clive, tell me what you're thinking behind those shut eyes of yours."

"First, I get a really strong feeling of wind upon my face. It's a cold wind, numbing. Beneath me, I see an icy grey ocean, the Atlantic. I feel borne upon the wind over rugged cliff-tops and sandy beaches. Through sheets of rain that batter the landscape, I see a ruined village on a hillside. Slowly, I am propelled toward the cottages and stone walls. Next to this village is an old, decrepit grave-yard. Rusted crosses protrude from the damp green surface. Eroded headstones are covered with brown mossy lichens, their worn inscriptions unreadable. A hooded figure is standing by an upturned tombstone. I think it's a woman. The figure is slender, tall. A cloak surrounds her. I cannot see her, her face lies deep within the hood. There is mystery here. I feel it, and yet something strange as well, sad and terrible. With pearl-white hands, she reaches to remove her hood and show her face. That's when I wake. Sometimes, I wake up screaming; other times, I wake up choking. This dream terrifies me, doctor. Still, I get comfort from graveyards. Figure that one out. Can you answer me that? Why the hell am I dreaming of Ireland, anyway? That was years ago!"

"Didn't you say your fascination with death began after your father died? When you were seven? Maybe you're stuck there. Have you heard of hypnosis?"

"Who hasn't? I've seen it on TV. You're going to dangle some medallion in front of me and send me into a trance, right?"

"That's the Hollywood take. In real life, hypnosis has been known to help anxiety, even addiction. At a stretch, in some cases it has been known to help recover memories a person may have blocked out. It might help you remember your childhood better. You've mentioned that the time of your father's death is blurred in your memory. Hypnosis could help. I think you should consider it."

"Sure, anything. I just want to get well and get out of here. You're on my side, aren't you, doctor? You won't let me alone in this, or plant anything in my head? God knows, I'm frightened enough."

"Clive, you've known me a long time now and, even though sometimes it's been tough, I'm sure you agree that I've never lied to you or deliberately harmed you in any way. You know you can trust me."

"Sorry, doc, that's my anxiety speaking. Let's give it a go. Something might give, eh?"

"All right, we'll give it a go. Ready?"

"Yeah, ready."

"I want you to look at the blue light on the top of this pen. I want you to focus on the light, look deep into the light. Focus on the blueness of the light... you are beginning to relax. Look deeper now into the light. You are drawn toward that light... the light is filling your mind with a gentle deep blue that floats on your thoughts. The colour is relaxing, reassuring, gentle, soft, warm...You are relaxing even more now, your mind is filled with this radiant blue light, it shines within you and fills the space around you. You are now totally relaxed...Your eyes close and the light fills you from within. You are drawn even deeper into the light, your body floating toward the centre, the core of the light. The core is a shining, glittering jewel within you, a sapphire, with many facets. You stare deep into the sapphire blue and see each surface of the jewel reflecting back on you. Look deeper on the surfaces of the blue, within each surface lies a picture from your past, a chapter in your life story.... I want you to look for the surface that shows you as a seven year-old-child, inside you see yourself. It is the night before your father died. I want you to float into that picture, float into that past, and when I count to three you are going to be there again, back when you were seven years old, back when you stopped remembering, One, two, three.

"Where are you?"

"Home, I just woken up. Room's dark. I can see my Batman on the wall. My eyes, dere sore, I was cryin'. Oh!"

"What's wrong, Clive? Why are you trembling?"

"Sometin' in de corner."

"What, Clive? What's there?"

"I want my Mam."

"Easy, Clive. There is no need to cry. Easy, it can't hurt you."

"White, combin' its long hayer."

"Easy now, Clive, tell me more."

"It's hurtin', sad. I'm sad. It's here for Daddy."

"Easy now, Clive. Easy, there's no need to tremble. You're safe."

"Still dere in de corner. I want to tell Daddy, I have to tell Daddy."

"Do you tell your Dad, Clive?"

"No, I'm scared. I'm under de covers now."

"OK, I want to take you forward a couple of minutes. Where are you now."

"Still hidin', under de covers."

"I'm going to take you..."

" AHHHHHHHH! It's dere, above me. It's floatin' down from de ceilin! Its face, its FAAACE! Mam, Daddy, its face. I'm tryna scream, I, I can't.

"Be brave, Clive, I think we are close to an answer. Tell me more, what does it say."

"Nutin. It's face is changin' fast, young, then old, then young again. It's telling me someten but it's not speakin'."

"What does it say, Clive. Tell me what does it say?"

"I hear it in my head, it's talkin' to me in me head."

"What is it saying, Clive? Clive, your voice is changing. Come back Clive!"

"I am born of the dead, come to journey another. Born to sorrow, I bring death among the living. I give you what I have not given in a thousand years. Choose, your father or you. Choose life, or journey with me. Choose sickness and suffering and toil or come with me now. Choose loss and grief or endless sleep. Choose. Your father or you. I wait, until you choose."

"I want my Da. My daddy, what can I do? I want to live! I want to live!"

"Clive, you're silent. What's happening?"

"My door is openin'. It's leavin'. It's turnin' to me in the doorway. It's tellin' me that... that one day it will come for me."

"OK, Clive, I am going to bring you out. I want you to move away from the light, back to your body, back to this room, I'm going to count to three. When I reach three, you will be awake."

"It's been following me since I got here. It's always been here. It wants me, it's been showing me Ireland, that's where it belongs, that is where it will take me, not to the living, but to the dead. It told me it would. It told me this day would come. It's my time. I can see the graveyard again. I see the figure cloaked in black, it's pulling back its hood. OH, OHH GOD! Its face, it's the same face!"

"One..."

"It's here now in this room. The same white face, the same long white hair, the same sharp strokes as it combs its hair. The same sadness. I don't want to die! Don't leave me alone in here with this thing! Daddy, I'm sorry. Daddy, don't leave me alone in here."

"Two..."

"What was I to do? I was only seven. I wanted to live, but I never did. I walked in graveyards all the time. I searched for my Daddy where I could. I thought I could bring him back. Yet, I knew that one day, it would find me. Oh God it's here! Its face pressed into mine, just like the night that Daddy died. It says it will hold me here forever, it says I must look upon its face forever. I'm trapped, Help me! Oh please, please, please, help me."

"Three. Clive? Clive? Wake up! Come on Clive, wake up! Shit, Clive wake up! Clive? Clive your eyes are open... I can feel your breathing...wake up, Clive, come on! Clive! Christ, come ON, Clive! Code yellow to ground floor, code yellow to ground floor."

"Hello, Mark? Mike here, calling you back. Look, I listened to the tape and reviewed the file. It doesn't seem to cover all of the case. Where did Clive spend his recovery? Did you have much trouble waking him up afterwards?

"Mike, Clive went catatonic, unresponsive, locked in his own mind. That's the thing. We could never get Clive out of it. He has never regained consciousness."

"What? That's not possible. I've never heard of a case like it."

"Well, you have now, and it's bothered me ever since. After the initial panic at St Margaret's was over, we moved him to Brigham and Women's. He lay catatonic for days. His body was asleep yet his eyes remained wide open. It has always looked to me like Clive is in a never-ending fright. In a never-ending state. We gave him a brain scan, you know. The results were totally abnormal for a catatonic. They indicated unusually high levels of brain wave activity. When we examined this closer, a pattern emerged which indicated that Clive's brainwave activity continued to spike at incredible levels for a number of seconds before dropping again. This would repeat itself over and over again for the duration of the scan. No matter how many times we performed the EEG, his brain always showed the same activity. When I had the results examined by a neuropsychologist, he informed me that the type of brain activity Clive was experiencing was, as I had already diagnosed, quite unusual for a person in a catatonic state. When I asked him why, he reluctantly told me this type of activity was consistent with someone who was screaming, over and over again."

"Christ, that's terrible, Mark."

"I know it is, and I've lived with it for twenty-five years. To this day Clive Sullivan lies in small cubicle at Brigham and Women's, forever screaming at something that will haunt him for whatever time his poor soul has left on this earth."

Lady Westropp's Gift

It was strange when it happened. I'd been lying awake in my South Boston bedroom ruminating about home. In the background, the wail of police sirens and the occasional call of a drunk filled the night with the usual irritating sounds of the city. Outside the Whitethorne the Irish were fighting again, living up to the stereotype in every way possible. In the meantime, I couldn't stop thinking.

For an emigrant, home is an elusive ever-present. It wasn't that my life in Boston was bad, it's just that it had been so much better in Ireland. It was true that since my wife and I had emigrated, we'd had some success, but what a struggle it's been, what a grind it is everyday. Life here is an endless blur of work, set against the backdrop of a cold, dirty inner city, where homeless people creep from the shelter of shop doorways asking for help that I can't give. I missed home. I missed the smells, I missed the light, and I missed the land in all its seasons.

Home was a paradox on which I would not stop ruminating, and night-time was when I ruminated most. In my trance-like state between sleep and wakefulness, I could gaze for hours out my bedroom window to the street light beyond. But of course I wasn't looking at the light. Instead, I saw again my old home and its surrounds, the bridge, the river, the castle above, and Heronswood house standing proudly overlooking the Owenabui valley, in that precious pastoral corner of south Cork. It's what every emigrant does late at night, I suppose, when his heart is torn between the living present and the sugar-coated memories of old. But I was different. I could almost touch home. I could feel it, smell it, taste it. It was as real to me as that street-light.

Then, one winter's night, rising from a sleepy slumber, I leaned toward my curtains to shut out the light that was so intrusive on my dreaming, when I slipped and fell, crashing on the dark of my bedroom floor. Yet, when I rose, I found myself sitting in the meadow behind my house in Ireland, under a gentle evening sun. From the lush green of the grass and the high growth of the hedgerows, I knew it to be mid June, a time when this particular conjunction of tiny fields was at its most beautiful. The scene brought a tear of joy to my eye. I was delighted that a dream, a bump on the head, or whatever it was, could be so vivid. I swooned in the ecstasy of this new reality. I sat listening to summer birds singing. I smelled the fresh cut grass on the warm gentle breeze and marvelled at the reddening sky as day turned to dusk and, after a time, I rose from my reverie and walked to my old house, enjoying this dream for what it was. Climbing the gate at the entrance to the field, I left the empty meadow and took my time strolling homeward.

The road ran down a sharp hill. In my absence new houses had sprung up along the road, houses that were bigger than the cottages of old or the modest bungalows that I had seen in my youth. These houses shadowed over the quaint old country lanes and struck a harsh contrast to the more gentle ancestral house of Heronswood and the castle at Dralane, structures which themselves seemed to blend into the landscape rather than oppress it. I realized that my home had changed, and, in doing so, I felt pangs of sadness. It was, I mused, the price an emigrant paid for being away.

Night drew in as I neared, and I noticed a light shining inside. I decided I would go in the back door. At least no one would see me that way, and I'd surprise them all. But the only face that greeted me was that of my mother, and tears were gathering in her eyes. She grasped a tissue and leaned forward in her chair, staring out the window of the front room. She stared and sobbed as I had never seen her do before.

"Ma? Mam? What's wrong, love?" I asked her. "Where is everyone? Why are you on your own?" But she didn't answer. Her vacant stare at the window was interrupted every so often by a sob. I felt a heavy burden upon her and begged her to talk, but my pleas made no difference. On the mantelpiece were a row of mass cards that reflected in the mirror behind. Just then another sob from my mother made me turn. Mam was curled in a foetal position on the edge of her chair. She let out an elongated keen before erupting into sobs again. Over and over, I tried to hug her, but she didn't respond. Even so, I held her fast until the worst of the sobs receded.

When Mam lay quite still, I decided to investigate. I walked throughout the house, but no one else was there. The rest of my family was gone, the rooms were empty, the house had grown mouldy from damp, and cracks had appeared along the bedroom walls and ceilings above. I went outside to the orchard behind and circled the house a few times. Then I returned and told Mam that I would be back when I had checked everything out. I was confused, a slight feeling of fear gathered in my stomach, and a gentle sweat broke out upon my forehead.

I walked to the humped-back bridge of Dralane, only yards from my childhood home. Night had fallen; a pale moon shone upon the river, casting a golden trail on the flowing waters that cascaded below the bridge and on to the weir beyond. I had often stood on this bridge on sultry summer nights, but tonight this part of home felt different. Above the river, where the dark conifers of the forest rose to meet the night sky, stood the castle of Dralane, a single light appearing in the window of a corner of the old ruin. It was a weak yellow dot adrift in a canvass of navy and black. Overall, the forest appeared smaller than I had known it, and around the river a great profusion of reed growth guarded the fringes of the riverbank, another feature I had never seen before. Silent echoes filled the night and reverberated around the small valley. A faint breeze blew through the reeds, creating a whispering that made me quite uneasy. A gentle footstep sounded behind me. I turned. In front of me, leaning against the low wall of the bridge, stood a young lady in Victorian costume.

She wore a long-sleeved dress, which in the moonlight was a pastel shade. On her head was a Victorian "dinner party" hat, the kind worn by ladies of the Gentry of old. She held a sketch book and had been busy at her work when I beheld her.

"A little dark for sketching, don't you think?" I asked.

She answered in a sweet mannered tone that seemed to hint of the gentry, a lilt that was almost English with a soft local inflection. "It depends what I wish to sketch. The half light of the moon can often suit a subject that is only half visible."

It took several moments before I babbled out the obvious question. "Are you sketching me?"

"Of course. I've sketched here for over a century. My drawings are quite good. They record what has been and what might have been in this tiny part of the universe."

"A century! What are you?" I asked.

She gave a gentle laugh. "Isn't it obvious, dear? I'm a ghost."

I was speechless, dumbfounded and steadfast in my disbelief. "No, you're not," I retorted. "I'm dreaming. I'll wake up in a minute."

Another girl-like giggle. "Oh, this is no dream." She giggled again. "I have a purpose tonight," she said. "I'm here to offer you a choice."

"I'm dreaming or I've bumped my head, but I'm still in my home, I'm still in Boston." I was distressed, frightened, unsure.

"No," she replied. "You are here. You are in between spaces. This is what the ancient Gaels might have called 'no time' or 'time out of time.' The rules are, shall we say, different here."

A cold sweat trickled down my back and added to my uncertainty. Even so, I decided to play the game, convinced that at some stage I would wake up.

"Fine," I replied. "Who are you? and why am I here?"

She replied in that faintly English voice, pleasant but firm. "I am Lady Westropp. A century ago I lived at Heronswood house on the hill above. As a young lady I loved to sketch from this bridge. It was always a place of refuge from the confines of a, shall we say, restricted household. Then I died. I've sat upon this bridge ever since, sketching the changes, marking the passing of things, of this place. I look for what is, what was, and, in your case, what might have been. I watched you grow from a lonely little boy fishing the riverbank to a youth with dreams of great things. I suppose you could say, I am the spirit of the place."

"But what is the point of all this?" I replied

"To show you what might have been, had you stayed here. Your past is finished, it will never return. But I can offer you a new existence, a chance to stay in the past you could have had, had you never left. You see, I saw you when you first walked here and noticed your nature. You were a sensitive child, open more than most to the beauty of this place, to its spirit. I noticed you were a timid boy, sad over the death of your father. So I enchanted you. In the depths of those Halloween nights when you listened to the song of the waters flowing underneath this bridge. I comforted you, healed you. In a way, I am in part responsible for your heartache. So I have decided to offer you a choice. Would you like to have stayed instead of leaving for America? Here, in this heaven you have created? Would you like to stay now? You can, if you want. This is my gift.

I shrugged my shoulders. "I can't desert my son. I have a wife and family now. They need me. I have commitments, miserable as some of them are. I just wish we had decided to stay here, that I had my family here. I don't know, I just wish I was something else other than muddled and sad."

"In that case, allow me to show you what would have become of you had you stayed here in Ireland. Look here," she said, and she walked toward me.

Just then the moon came out and shone brightly upon her face. The woman's face changed from the lovely countenance of a young lady to brown leathery skin from which two pale eyes loomed out from underneath her dinner hat. In her hand she held open her sketch book, and on it I could see clearly a drawing of the bridge on which we stood, its three arches resplendent in moonlight above a swollen river that rushed underneath.

"Look closer," she commanded.

I leaned down and beheld the figure of a man suspended in mid air above the river beneath the apex of the middle arch.

"Closer," she repeated.

I stared hard at the picture until the image of a slender line running from the bridge above to the man's neck almost seemed to jump out of the canvass at me. With a gasp I saw the man's slanted head and beheld the noose fastened around his neck. At precisely that moment, the wind gusted across the sketch book, an effect which made the paper shimmer and for a moment I thought I saw the figure in the drawing sway from side to side while dangling above the rushing water.

I turned my face away in disgust. "There has never been a suicide on this bridge," I shouted at her. "In all the years I lived here, this never happened!"

Again came the faint lilting voice, "Who are you to say? This is what certainly did happen, to you, if you had stayed here in Ireland."

"Give me that thing." I pulled the sketchbook from her hands and flipped through the pages. Over and over again I searched the book's images, images that were at times too terrible to mention, terrible because in every one of them, I was dead. Dead in a myriad of monstrous alternative ways. And then, the wind caught the pages again and the moon shone bright above the bridge of Dralane, and while the wind blew, the pages turned in rapid succession. They turned so fast that the images began to move like the awakening of some terrible cartoon, except in this cartoon, I was the star. And in each frame, I saw how my life, the life of my family, would have been had I stayed. I saw our early success, my success. First a bright beginning, a thriving business, a new house, a car, holidays in the sun. Then came the changes, an economic crash, the business failing, the repossession of our house, my spiral into depression, my marriage ending, my family taken from me. I realised that I had failed, failed at my relationships, failed at life. I saw each scenario play out, one misfortune after another, each building upon the next, each leading to greater sorrow until abruptly the turning stopped and I beheld the figure, my figure, my body, swaying above the waters of the Owenabui.

"Now you know," she said. "If you had stayed you would be dead and your mother driven insane with grief. You did the right thing when you left."

I dropped to my knees in a pitiful childish gesture. This home I had loved so much, this hidden gem of beauty, this tiny river valley – all of it was part of my soul and yet it had been right, somehow right, to leave. I couldn't face it, I didn't want to face it, I turned angrily to whatever this demon was and told her quiet plainly, "You are lying."

No sooner had I uttered my contempt when black coiled wires shot from the darkness behind Lady Westropp. One wrapped itself around my neck while the other pulled heavily on my feet. With a queasy sense of horror, I saw that the wire around my feet was attached to a heavy stone, a stone meant for only one thing, to stretch my neck until it broke. Then I was being dragged towards the wall of the bridge. I gasped in a sickly effort to scream. I grabbed out, tearing at anything that I could hold onto. My fingers scraped and scored the ancient stones of the bridge, but it was all in vain. Up and over the wall I toppled, my body falling into space, my mind erupting in an agonizing screech that no one heard. Down I went, rushing headlong toward the dark waters below, knowing that any time soon, a terrible crack would sever my spine and my body would right itself to dangle beneath the bridge as Lady Westropp had shown me. But the crack never came.

Instead, I awoke on my bedroom floor in Boston. The light was now illuminating the entire room. My wife lay sleeping gently on her side. In the crib on the other side of the room, my baby son lay sleeping. I leaned over and kissed his cheek as I had never done before. Then I got into bed and wrapped my arms round my wife. I kissed her gently behind the ear and softly, ever so softly, I gave thanks to Lady Westropp for her gift. I gave thanks for the very real and tangible treasures in my life, and not the mournful dreams and remembrances of an island far far away.

Eoghain Hamilton is originally from Carrigaline, County Cork. He now lives in Boston, Massachusetts with his wife and son.